BB Guns
Remembered

Tom Gaylord

Gaylord Communications, Inc.

Other books by Tom Gaylord—*The Beeman R1 Supermagnum Air Rifle*, © 1995 by GAPP, Inc.

For Edith

Acknowledgements

The author wishes to acknowledge the late airgun collector Marvel Freund for providing the photograph used in the *Reminiscing* chapter. It was that photo that started the work on this book.

Thanks are also given to noted airgun collector Wes Powers for providing most of the other vintage images used in this book.

Thanks to Stephen Larsen, who provided the illustrations for *The wind gun of Prostl*.

The author thanks airgun builder Gary Barnes of Barnes Pneumatic Arms for providing the insight and background for the chapter titled *The wind gun of Prostl*. The challenges of building an outside lock airgun were seen more clearly through Gary's eyes.

Finally my thanks to Elaine Lanmon of Just Ink Digital Design. She did the interior layout and the cover design, plus assisted the author with many fundamental questions a new writer has. Without her, there would be no book.

Table of Contents

Chapter 1 – Reminiscing...7

Chapter 2 – Andy 13

Chapter 3 – Chicken Dinner 19

Chapter 4 – Squirrel boy 27

Chapter 5 – My Quackenbush..33

Chapter 6 – Never let her down 43

Chapter 7 – How I bought my BB gun 51

Chapter 8 – Long time coming 61

Chapter 9 – Little Chief 69

Chapter 10 – By the book 75

Chapter 11 – Straight shooter 85

Chapter 12 – Values...95

Chapter 13 – Young hunter...101

Chapter 14 – Howard 109

Chapter 15 – The wind gun of Prostl.................................117

Chapter 1

Reminiscing

This photograph was given to me by a good friend and fellow airgun enthusiast. He bought the original somewhere, then had it reproduced and enhanced to what you see here.

The picture stopped me cold when I first saw it. Who were these boys? Where did they get those BB guns? When was this picture taken; and by whom? What was the occasion?

Then I had a thought. The picture might suggest a short story. It would be completely fanciful, of course, but it might not be that far off the money, either. With apologies to whoever these boys turned out to be, I submit the following.

Oh, that was the summer of 1907. I had just celebrated my second birthday party out at the farm. The folks were just glad that I was alive, after the accident, so it was a bigger celebration than I realized at the time—but I guess that's true of any kid's birthday. I was just glad to get out of the city and play where there were no restraints. Nobody told you not to go into the street on the farm because there weren't any streets. There weren't even very many paths out there, and I could run all over the lawn without getting yelled at by my mother every five minutes.

My older cousin Vernon had taken me out to the kitchen garden to shoot his BB guns. He had to cock them for me, but he let me shoot them at some tin cans he set up on the old wooden wheelbarrow at the end of the garden. I don't remember if I actually hit any or not. I was too wrapped up in my hero worship of Vernon. Of all the boys in Aunt Lucy's family, he was the one who always made time for me. When I was older, he used to take me down to the pond, where the two of us would catch a mess of brim for our supper. Vernon would clean them and then we would fry them over an open fire on green willow holders he made right there.

But it was the BB guns I remember the most. Vernon always had two or three around the place and I was welcome to shoot any of them. Since our house was in town, my folks wouldn't let me have a gun until I was well into my teens, so the 10-mile train ride out to Vernon's farm got to be a weekly occurrence after I got a little older.

Vernon used to fix all the county kids' BB guns for them, and occasionally he would swap one of his for something else. I got to see Hexagons, Bijous, Matchless, Daisys, Kings, and even some of the old all-wood Chicago guns. The wire-stock Daisys were the best, if you shot them with lead BB shot. Vernon had a whole bag of it in his shed, so there was never a time we didn't have something to shoot. I had to promise not to tell the other kids where he kept it, though, or the bag would have disappeared pretty quickly.

When I got my first .22 in 1921, it was Vernon who showed me how to shoot it. My pop took me out once on the day I got it, but it was Vernon who was there the rest of the time. I was allowed to take it on the train out to the farm, as long as I kept it in the green canvas bag that came with it.

We used to go out into the fields on the farm and the neighboring place, too, and shoot at woodchucks and crows. Aunt Lucy would give us a nickel for every crow we brought her, because she said they were "good crows" that wouldn't get into her corn anymore. You could buy a box of shorts for fifteen cents at the hardware store near my house, so all you had to do was shoot three crows for your next box. That was when I got my bright idea.

Daisy had come out with the model 25 pump BB gun, which was the most powerful BB gun we had ever seen. If we could kill a crow with that, we would be in tall cotton, because you could buy a whole tube of lead BBs for three cents! There must have been thousands of BBs in one of those tubes—or at least that's how it seemed. The problem was how to get one of those BB guns.

As I recall, they sold for over four dollars in the store, so buying one new was out. No kid I knew ever had more than a dollar and a half. If you did, your folks made you put it in the bank. Funny thing about that was, you could put your money in the bank real easy, but there was no way you could get it out again! Your parents had to tell the bank it was okay, and there was no way that was going to happen.

I told Vernon about my idea, and he seemed to warm to it. The two of us schemed for a couple of days and came up with a plan. We would have to find a kid who had a model 25 and trade him out of it. But that proved next to impossible, because every kid wanted a 25 over all other BB guns. No amount of marbles, folding knives, compasses, horseshoe puzzles or carnival prizes could get one of these most-coveted guns out of its lucky owner's tight grasp. Heck, you had to give them something just to hold their gun for awhile. Vernon even tried offering some of his strange old BB guns, but no dice.

So, on an impulse, I offered one of them my .22 in trade. Well, did THAT ever stop the train on the tracks! A .22 for a BB gun! It was unheard of! The .22 was every kid's dream. Even a lowly single shot, which mine was, was the most prized possession you could have. The news of this offer spread all over the neighborhood within a few hours.

It didn't take the kid very long to make up his mind, either. He wanted to see my gun first, which I thought was fair; but when he said he wanted to shoot it, I drew the line. If he got to shoot mine, I also got to shoot his. Five shots of his for one of mine seemed fair, because these were .22 rounds, after all.

We went down to the creek, traded shots and finally, to everyone's utter disbelief, we swapped our guns. He was beaming, but I knew I had got the better deal because now I could shoot crows for next to nothing, to raise money for….

And that's when it hit me! I was wanting to shoot crows to get money to buy more .22 rounds. What was I thinking? I'd traded off a gun I had been struggling to support to get a gun I could use to raise money to support the gun I traded off! I had never been so low as when the reality of the situation finally hit me.

Vernon heard about the incident after it happened, and he didn't say very much. I think he knew how low I felt, and anything he could have said would make me feel even lower. Because of my unwillingness to talk about it, the trade was soon forgotten, although I never broke the news to my folks, because the .22 had been a special present.

In the late '20s, Vernon started doing gunsmithing work for Old Man Hochstaadt, the owner of the hardware store near my house. In a few years, he had a small corner of the store set up with guns for sale, and, in 1934, he bought the whole store from Hochstaadt's widow.

I went off to war as a correspondent in 1942, and I was in the Pacific Theater in 1944 when the letter came from home telling me of Vernon's death. He had been caught in a fire when the sugar house burned down out at the farm. It was during maple sugar time, and he was supposed to keep the boiler stoked while the others gathered the buckets of sap. They sent me a picture of his tombstone and I cried for two days.

After I returned to the States in 1947, Aunt Lucy asked me out to the farm one final time. She was in her late 70s and couldn't see well enough to be by herself, so she was going to sell the place and move to town. She handed me a cardboard box wrapped with red paper and a card she told me Vernon had written after I shipped out.

The card read, "Jimmy, I found this at an auction sale last week and I thought of you." Inside the box was a well-worn Winchester model '03 with the initials J.T. carved under the grip. I remembered carving them there the day I got the rifle in 1921. Aunt Lucy also gave me five old BB guns, including a beautiful Daisy model 25 that I recognized as my own. She told me Vernon had wanted to see the look on my face when he gave them to me after the war.

Then Aunt Lucy gave me one last thing—a faded cracked

photograph she had taken of me and Vernon standing by the kitchen garden wall on my second birthday. She told me that I had always been his favorite cousin and that she knew I loved him as much as he loved me. He wasn't even remorseful about the time a year earlier, when he had to pull me out of my buggy after my carriage rolled out on the railroad tracks.

Chapter 2
Andy

When I was just a young fellow, my family used to spend the summer on Kelly's Island in Lake Erie. There were summer cabins, and families would rent them by the week or month. Our family often spent the whole summer out there, with my dad taking the ferry to Sandusky, where he caught the train to his office in Cleveland during the week. On Friday evening, he would join us at the cabin, and we would all be together until the evening ferry left again on Sunday.

My sisters and I pretty much had the run of the island during the week. As long as the weather was good, we could swim or look for shells along the gravelly beach. I would sometimes go fishing with Tom Johnson, who had the place next to ours, but he was a lot older and liked to stay out in his rowboat all day, which I found boring. So, I suppose I went swimming on most days or just went over to look at the glacial moraines carved in the bedrock. The island was full of them. Huge gray rocks with deep grooves cut into them by glaciers or something.

But my favorite time of all was spending time with Andy. He was one year older, and his family lived in New York City. They usually got to the island around the middle of June and stayed until Labor Day, just like us. Andy's father even stayed the whole time, too.

Andy was so interesting because he always had a different perspective on things. When I told him about the circus my folks took me to in the fall, he told me about something called an amusement park that was set up all the time in New York. It sounded like a circus and a carnival rolled up in one, but it also had some things I had never heard of. Like a roller coaster. Andy said they had the biggest roller coaster in the world at Coney Island, and he tried to describe it to me. Years later, when I finally saw one for myself, I could see he hadn't exaggerated. At the time, though, I wasn't too sure.

Another thing he told me was that in New York the kids could not have any kind of guns. Now, I could see why they couldn't have .22s, because you couldn't shoot them in Cleveland, either, but he said it went further than that. He said even BB guns were frowned on by officials, and, if a cop saw a kid with one, he would confiscate it. That seemed pretty extreme to me, but it did explain why he was so attached to his Daisy. It seems that he only got to use the gun out at the island, so that was what he did whenever he came. He didn't swim; he didn't fish. He just used to grab that gun of his in the morning and carry it all around the island all day long. As a result, Andy got to be a pretty good shot.

I had a Columbian BB gun back home in Euclid, so I wasn't as fascinated as he was. I could shoot practically any time I wanted to, so I guess I got my fill of it. I did bring it with me to the island, but I didn't shoot it all the time. There was swimming and fishing and exploring and picnics and all sorts of other good stuff to do out there.

But Andy was different. He just shot and shot all day long. His folks were loaded, so there was never a problem with having enough shot. I suppose he had several 5-lb. sacks of BBs when he got to the island, and I'm sure he never went home with any. He would even loan me some when I ran out, which happened weekly. Dad would always bring a few tubes with him on Friday, but I was out by the following Wednesday, and I didn't want to push my luck. So, I borrowed from Andy.

Andy had a nickname for me. It was Tovarik. He said that was the name of one of his best friends back home. I sort of went along with it, although it seemed a little strange. He never called me that in front of my folks; but when we were alone, I was Tovarik all the time.

Sometimes, we went camping. Just the two of us and Andy's dad. He was a real swell guy, too. Not like other fathers, I guess he didn't have to work because he used to do the same stuff us kids did, and he seemed to have just as much fun.

He had a thick accent, which my dad said sounded European to him. I never paid much attention because, in those days, every other adult had some kind of accent. But, Andy's dad could tell the greatest stories whenever we would get him alone. He told us about kings and emperors and armies and wars and all kinds of neat stuff like that. He said when he was a little boy, his dad used to take him camping and fishing at some island very much like Kelly's island, but in his home country.

And, he liked to shoot as much as Andy. I watched the two of them snipe at pine nuts from 40 feet, a range I would have said was beyond even the best BB guns. They connected with a lot of those shots, so you couldn't say it was just luck. I tried to keep up, but I seldom connected. Not like those two, for sure.

I remember one time very well. We were all out camping near the end of the season, and Andy wanted to take a shot at a crow high up in a tree. His dad wouldn't let him because he said the BB would only hurt the bird and not kill it. That's when he told both of us, "If you ever shoot at a living creature, make sure you kill it on the first shot. There is no reason to make an innocent animal suffer for your lack of good sportsmanship."

That's when I asked him, "But what if you are shooting at a criminal? Or an enemy soldier? Shouldn't you shoot them, no matter what?" In those days, the books we read were full of tales about how some kid our age got mixed up with criminals and his own good marksmanship bailed him out at the end. Often, it was as good to simply wound the bad guy as to actually kill him, or at least that's what the stories said.

I'll never forget what Andy's father told me. He said, "Never leave an enemy alive. They will only recover to come after you again. If you shoot an enemy, always make sure he's dead." The look in his eyes when he said that was enough to chill my blood. I knew the man wasn't just saying it; he meant it. I think he even lived it.

I never told my folks about that because they were already suspicious of Andy's dad as it was. My mom and dad often talked about him when they thought I was asleep. They wondered where his money came from and why he had so much time on his hands. My mom thought he was a criminal of some sort, but my dad was sure he was just some sort of European with money, like a banker or something.

When I turned 16, I stopped going out to the island because my folks enrolled me in preparatory school, which took that summer as well as one full school year. After that, I was accepted at West Point, where I attended and finally graduated. Mom and my sisters still went out to the island each summer, until my older sister got married. Then they started staying nearer to home, and eventually my middle sister got married as well.

Dad retired from his legal practice and he and mom bought a smaller home, now that us kids were out of the house. I still went back for visits, but the carefree days on Kelly's island shooting BB guns with Andy had faded into dim memories.

Then the Great War started in Europe, and, as I was serving in the Army, I was certain to go if we got in. Training took up all my time until the day came when Mr. Wilson finally gave the word to go "Over There." I served in France and was gassed early in my first campaign, so I got the free trip home to recover in a hospital in New York. I thought about Andy, as I was finally in his city, but I didn't have the slightest notion of how to find him. I didn't even know his last name!

But, as things sometimes do, it worked out completely different than I expected. Andy found me. Or at least I learned where he had been since our happy days on the island. In 1921, I saw his picture in an article in the paper, with about thirty other people I didn't know. It seems his whole family had been executed in Russia when the Bolsheviks took over. You see, Andy's last name was Romanof, and that cost both him and his father their lives. That was when I finally understood what his father had meant about enemies.

But the story doesn't end there. It ends in 1925, when I bought a nickel-plated Daisy BB gun in a second-hand shop in Cleveland. There was no doubt that it was Andy's old gun because he had scratched his name in the metal wire of the stock. Only now my mature eyes read the name Andrei R.

Isn't it funny how the little things in life often turn out to be the biggest, only we don't find out about them until it's over?

Chapter 3
Chicken dinner

In the first part of the 20th century, outings were an important part of American life. Magazine articles, newspaper accounts and even whole books were written proclaiming the benefits of enjoying the healthy outdoors life. Outdoor equipment was in high demand, and entire catalogs were devoted to displaying the finest grades of sporting dry goods and equipment. Companies like Abercrombie & Fitch ruled the day, and young boys, especially, looked forward to the day when they could be properly outfitted for whatever adventures might come their way. So it was with me.

I lived in New Jersey, and the opportunity for outings into the wilderness were usually restricted to local parks or the seashore. The parks were fun, but you could easily walk out of their boundaries in a few hours, and the New Jersey coastline was as well developed in those days as it is today. So, a fellow had to read stories and do a lot of daydreaming if he wanted adventure.

One day, however, all that changed for me. My uncle, Don, on my mother's side, was a naturalist who worked for National Geographic magazine. He was always off exploring faraway lands and sending back Kodaks of his adventures. I idolized him, which I guess he suspected, because whenever he would come to visit us, I monopolized as much of his time as I could. On one such visit, he surprised both me and my parents by offering to let me accompany him on his next journey.

He was going to explore the ancient lands of the Mandan Indian tribe of North Dakota to document what had become of the tribe since they were first contacted by Lewis & Clark. Since the trip was to be inside the United States and since it was only scheduled to last three weeks, he won permission to take me along. I would miss some school, but my father said the experience would help to round out my education more than long division and diagramming sentences. Since he was also the principal of the school I attended, there was no need for further discussion on that subject.

I might note that my mother was concerned about my getting bored, being in the field with her brother all that time. "It won't be like the park, Jamie. You won't be able to come home when you get tired. If you go, you'll have to stay the full time until your uncle is ready to come home." That actually worried me, as I had no idea what life would be like in the field. I imagined hunting big game and fishing for salmon; but, to hear Uncle Don, it was more like a day on the farm. I wasn't sure how I'd feel after several weeks of it. Still, I wanted to go, if only to find out what it was like to be in the field.

To get me ready for the trip, my father and uncle took me into New York City to the famous Abercrombie & Fitch store downtown, where they bought me a full set of expedition clothes and camping equipment. Since we were there, I was allowed to look at the guns they had on display in their famous gun room. Wall after wall of beautiful walnut-stocked rifles and shotguns from the most famous makers in the world. The brief time we spent in that room was the single most fascinating moment of my young life.

We left New Jersey by train in mid-April and traveled to Bismark, North Dakota, where my uncle hired a car. Our drive to the Mandan site was over some very rustic trails and sometimes even over open ground. I wasn't sure the flivver could make it, but my uncle seemed to know exactly where we were going. It was farm country now, and we were on a huge farm that he had obtained permission from before the trip.

When we finally got where we were going, he located a good place for our camp and we set about to make ourselves "at home." There were some outbuildings nearby, but he wanted to stay away from them. So we camped on the opposite side of a small pond. That was when I learned of my biggest surprise.

After the tent was up and the campfire was going, Uncle Don called me over to have a pow-wow with him. He told me he was going to be very busy in the coming weeks and I would have to take care of the camp for him. I was thrilled to think he would trust me to do that, but that was before I found out all that it meant. Not only was I to keep the fire going all day and night, he also wanted me to haul water, cover the waste pit and provide some of our rations. I had brought my fishing pole and the small pond near where we were set up looked good, but he said he wanted more than just fish.

From the back of his trunk he produced a long narrow cardboard box that had an exciting look to it. I knew what sort of things came in such boxes because I spent all my time looking at them in the local stores at home. This was a gun box! Only, this wasn't just any gun box. It had an Abercrombie & Fitch label on the cover, so I figured he had gotten it when we were there.

"Jaime," he said, "I want you to hunt for us with this gun. This land abounds with the famed prairie chicken, and I would like to eat some while we are here. So I am giving you this gun to use."

That word "use" struck me as odd. Why buy a new gun, only to loan it to me? Why not just borrow one of my father's many rifles? Why buy a new one? Then, he told me.

"This is a BB gun. I want you to use it because it makes very little noise, so I won't be distracted while I work. Also, the BB doesn't carry as far as a bullet, so I think you are old enough to be trusted to use it on your own. We don't want any of the farmer's cattle dropping over suddenly from lead poisoning, now do we?"

I don't remember what I said to that. Although I didn't actually own a BB gun, many of my friends did and I had used them enough to know what to do. Besides, my father had already taught me how to use a real gun the year before, so there wasn't much fear that I would do anything unsafe. But then, Uncle Don said something that took me by complete surprise.

"If you manage to provide me with a bird dinner at least five nights while we are here, I'll give that gun to you with my thanks." As far as I was concerned, Uncle Don had just given away a BB gun.

Then, I got my first lesson in prairie chickens. They don't abound and you could never get close enough to one to shoot it with a BB gun, even if they did. For the next three days I hunted high and low for the elusive birds and was always disappointed. They are the wariest creatures on God's green earth.

Using your best approach, the closest you can get to a prairie chicken is about 100 feet. That's well beyond the striking distance of any BB gun. They run along the ground just in front of you and then flutter a few yards if you try to overtake them. After some trials around camp, I learned that I would have to get within about 25 to 30 feet if I wanted to have a chance of bagging one. I thought my uncle had given me an impossible task.

On the third night at the evening meal, he remarked to me, "See many chickens, today?"

I said that I had, and proceeded to tell him about their discouraging habit of keeping just in front of me.

"What you should do is what the Mandans used to do when they wanted some. They used bows to get theirs, and a bow doesn't have much range, either. So, you know what they learned to do?"

I was all ears at this point. My uncle was gong to tell me how to bag a chicken with a BB gun.

"They used to put grain out for the birds to eat. Then they'd hide nearby and shoot them when they came to eat."

What a wonderful idea? Grain as bait. Only, we didn't have any grain with us. Then I thought about the rice we had in a sack. Rice is a grain. Maybe the birds would like rice.

The whole next day I tried baiting prairie chickens with piles of rice. The only thing I could tell for sure after that was they don't like rice. In fact, I think they hate it. I would have been really disappointed that evening at dinner if I hadn't noticed something late in the day. A whole flock of the elusive chickens were down at the edge of the pond, pecking for something in the bushes. I never saw what it was, but I reasoned that as long as I knew where they were, it didn't matter why they were there. I dodged Uncle Don's questions that evening and set about to plan my attack the next day.

What I was going to do was build a hide in the bushes near where I had seen the chickens feeding the evening before. I tried to build a brush pile hide, but there wasn't enough brush around to make one. The country hadn't begun to bloom that spring, and the amount of heavy brush was disappointing. But there was something even better.

Near the edge of the pond was an old rowboat that must have been used for fishing. I turned it upside down and made a very cozy hide along the edge of the pond just a few feet from where the birds had been the evening before. Sure enough, as the sun was getting low in the western sky, they began coming over to feed. I had a clear shot at them from less than 20 feet away.

In all, I managed to get three birds that evening. I would have gotten more but my uncle's yelling for me to come to dinner scared the flock off. Instead of taking all three birds to camp, I cleaned them all but hid two under the boat to bring home the next evening if I wasn't as lucky.

My uncle was stunned that I even got one prairie chicken! He said he thought it was next to impossible to bag one with a BB gun. I almost broke down and showed him the other two, but I really wanted to get that BB gun and to get it I had to provide at least five chicken dinners. We only had six nights left on the trip, so I wasn't about to overfeed him on one night just to lose my gun!

I needn't have worried. The next evening, I bagged four birds and the night after that two more, plus a little rabbit. We had chickens all over the camp in various stages of preparation. I had a sack full of feathers and down plus a rabbit skin, and my uncle was beside himself with amazement! In all, I shot 13 birds, three rabbits and a field mouse. Needless to say, I got my BB gun at the journey's end.

When we returned home, my uncle told my parents the whole story of the chickens all over again, making it sound like I was Jungle Jim or something. I was so swelled up with pride over my accomplishment that I finished the school year on a cloud.

Thirty years later, I asked my uncle to tell me about that trip once again. He didn't say much. He just smiled and said, "That two dollar BB gun was the best baby-sitter I ever had. You were so caught up in hunting those damn birds that the days just flew by for you."

I hadn't thought about it that way, of course, but upon reflection I see what he did. That's why I bought each of my boys a Daisy for their first outing with their dad. They should learn how to eat chicken dinners.

Chapter 4

Squirrel boy

BB guns? No, I never had much use for them. I always had a soft spot in my heart for the really powerful air rifles from Benjamin and

Crosman. You know the ones—you pumped them up and they shot like a .22. Well, almost as hard.

I had a few traditional BB guns as a young kid, but they were never of much interest to me because the darn things were so weak. Most of them could only dent a tin can at close range, and even the more powerful ones weren't all that strong. But there was one exception.

My first Benjamin was one of the old types that had the pump rod in the front of the gun. You pulled it out and then pushed down on the whole gun with the pump handle resting against something hard. Don't use tree roots, though; they're too slippery. You'll get almost down and the doggone handle will slip and you'll have to do the whole thing over. After a few pumps the lead BB was dropped down the muzzle and it would jam in the barrel until you shot.

I think I got that gun around 1919 or so. The war was over in Europe and people were back to their normal lives once again. I hawked newspapers in downtown Akron every day after school, so I always had some dough to spend. When I saw that gun in the sporting goods department at O'Neil's, I just knew I had to have it. The salesman told me I could control the power by the number of pumps I put in. Three was good enough for most shooting, but four was for really long shots, or for bigger game. The guy said that five pumps were even possible, but it took a whole lot of strength and if the gun was pumped that many times, it would shoot like a .22. That's what sold me. I wanted a gun that shot like a .22 but didn't cost a fortune for bullets. With a .22, you paid fifteen cents for about 25 shots, or so.

In those days, lead BBs cost five cents for a huge bag that lasted for weeks. Because my gun needed to be pumped up each time it was shot, I went through the bag even slower than a kid with a regular BB gun would have. I was in hog heaven, shooting for a fraction of the price a regular .22 rifle would have cost. That's always good when a guy has to come up with the money himself.

I bought that gun, but I had to keep it out of sight at home because we lived in the city and my folks would have pitched a fit if they knew I had it. BB guns were okay, but a gun that was, in essence, a .22, was an entirely different matter. They would have been worried about me shooting through walls and stuff like that, so I just kept mum about the whole thing.

I hid my gun out in the garage behind a box next to the wall, and I kept some of the shot in a bag in my paper sack. On weekday evenings in the summer, I would take it to the vacant lots near our house and shoot at squirrels in the trees. It was hard to hit them, but I managed it a time or two when I got close enough. They always dropped in their tracks with a good head shot.

One of my friends had a shooting range in his back yard and a lot of kids brought their guns over to have a try at it. His old man had hung big spoons and paint can lids in the tree branches and we could shoot at them as long as we liked because there was nobody living behind their property.

I remember one time a lot of us guys were shooting over there and the kid's dad who built the range came out to see what we were doing. He wanted to try all our guns so, of course, we let him. When he came to mine everyone warned him how powerful it was. Someone even blabbed that it was as powerful as a .22 on five pumps, so he said he believed he'd like to see that. We couldn't very well shoot a .22 on his property, because they were just as much in town as my folks were, so he said we could go over to the city dump on Saturday. There it was okay to shoot .22s, and of course my gun as well.

So, we all loaded up in his truck on Saturday and went over to test the gun. When we got there, he lined up six tin cans at 25 feet and shot clean through all of them with his .22 Remington. Then it was my turn. I lined up another six cans of about the same size and shot into the front one. The lead BB didn't even completely go through the front of that can, to say nothing of the ones behind. Boy, did I ever feel like a jerk! I guess I said something, but there was nothing I could say after bragging on my gun like that and then being shown up. I had believed the guy in the store, or at least I wanted to believe him so much that I kept repeating what I knew to be a lie. I guess that's what a real sales job can do.

After the big question had been answered, we hung around the dump for a while and shot rats. I got six and my friend and his dad shot about 20 with their Remington. I think they felt sorry for me, except the father said he was impressed that my gun would kill a rat. I told him about all the squirrels I had killed in the vacant lot by my house, but my story lacked conviction, now that I had been proved a liar.

He was interested, though. Real interested. He said he had a nest of squirrels in his attic that he had done everything to remove, but nothing worked. He couldn't shoot them with a .22 because the bullet could go right through the boards on the outside of the house, where it might injure someone. A regular BB gun was also out of the question because it would only injure the squirrels without killing them. He wondered if I might possibly come over and give him a hand with them.

That same evening, I cleaned out five gray squirrels from that man's attic rafters. It was like a zoo in there. I dropped every one of them with five pumps in the gun. The lead BB went in one side of the head and stayed there. No danger to anything else.

The man was so grateful that he offered to give me a dollar for the job, but I turned him down. After the embarrassment at the dump, I just wanted to get out of there with a little self-respect.

The next evening, a man came by our house and asked to speak to me. He had a big house on the other side of town and there was a squirrel problem in his attic. Would I please come over and help?

I did, and he was so happy with the job that he gave me a silver dollar. After that, I was asked several times a month to clean out attics all over Akron. People would pay me as much as fifty cents a squirrel for the job, and it was worth it because those animals were notorious for starting fires when they gnawed through the insulation on electrical wires.

My parents began to think of me as the "squirrel boy" because that's how people who didn't know me would ask for me. I didn't have to hide my gun any longer, not because it wasn't powerful after all, but because it was so popular. I even got my picture in the Akron Beacon Journal for killing squirrels in attics, and the popularity after that led to my going into business full time. I gave up my paper job and had business cards printed up to tell people of my services. I soon found that my best customers were not the actual homeowners, but insurance agents who told their clients to use me to lower their fire rates.

I did that work straight through high school, after which I went into the extermination business full time. I didn't just get rid of squirrels any more—I did the whole spectrum of pests. My business grew very well, and as I added each new exterminator, he always got a Benjamin air rifle to take care of the larger critters. My own Benjamin was mounted on a plaque in my office until I sold the business in 1953, when I took it with me.

How about that? An airgun that proved to be an embarrassment in the beginning actually defined the rest of my adult life. On reflection, I guess I'd say I like BB guns a lot.

Chapter 5
My Quackenbush

Although my family was from New York where I was born, I grew up in Mission San Jose in California in the 1880s. The schools were primitive at that time, so I stopped going when I was fifteen, having gone as far as possible in our little community.

California was such a wild place in those early days. There were still plenty of old 49ers around and they would tell you their story (or any story) with little encouragement. I listened to them all, because they were the most interesting entertainment we had. Tales of Joachin Murietta and Black Bart the Po-8, and how they rampaged through the gold fields around Mokalumne and Hangtown. Many of the old gentlemen were inveterate liars, having only recently arrived in the territory and therefore knew as little as I did, but every once in awhile I got to meet the real thing—some crusty old hardtack panner who had lived through the days of the famous gold rush. The stories they told made the impostors worth the trouble.

My family started a small orchard of plum and pear trees just outside of town. We bought 160 acres from a Mr. Campbell, who told us the land was ideal for fruit trees, and, indeed it was. Of course you don't start picking fruit from first year trees, so we also planted an acre of strawberries, which can be picked as early as the second year. We also raised several vegetable crops like lettuce, corn, squash and beans. It was those crops that sustained us those first few years while the orchard grew.

I was the general farmhand of the place. I had two younger brothers and a sister, and together the four of us worked on that farm as hard as the draft animals. But it wasn't all work. My father knew what it took to raise more than just crops, and he had us kids doing things we liked to do along with the rest of the chores.

My brother Bobby was the family fisherman and my special job was pest eliminator. I had to get rid of the thieving pigeons and rats that threatened our corn crib. For the job, I got to use a Quackenbush air rifle, perhaps the only one of its kind in the territory. Father had bought it in Herkimer before we left New York, and he said it was a good investment, since cartridges cost so much in California.

I could drop a rat from twenty feet away with that gun. All it took was a head shot. Sometimes they weren't completely dead when I got to them, but I dispatched them as quickly as I could.

The pigeons were a different story. They could take a direct shot and fly away as if nothing had happened. They were always a little farther than the rats, because of the way the place was laid out, but I still figured that a bird would have gone down before a rat!

Then I met an old-timer who changed everything. His name was Scrappy Jack Hill and he had been there since before color was found in Sutter's mill race. He had come out from Kentucky to build a new life, but the rush got in the way and he allowed himself to get caught up in it. As he often said to me, "If you don't take advantage of life when it deals you a winning hand, you might as well get out of the game."

Scrappy Jack claimed to have stashed a small fortune in gold and silver that he prospected during the rush. He said it was up in the hills between our valley and the Pacific Ocean, which was only a few days ride away. He often talked about going back up there to make a withdrawal from his "bank," as he called it.

I didn't completely believe him, as he was mostly a beggar in our village. But every so often, he would disappear for several weeks then reappear with new clothes and a fresh horse or mule. He always said he got lucky at the faro tables in San Francisco, but I wondered about that.

One day I happened to tell Scrappy Jack about the problem the pigeons were causing me at the farm. He asked to see my gun, and when I showed it to him, he acted like a little kid a Christmas. He had never seen something like that Quackenbush, nor had anybody else west of the Mississippi, I'd wager. I think he thought I was going to show him some old .22 rifle or something.

Well, he said he simply had to have that air rifle of mine. He wanted it the way some people want things—so much he couldn't think of anything else. I definitely didn't want to sell it to him, but I didn't see what else I could do as he was making such a fuss.

My father told me to set a real high price, and that might discourage the old fellow, so I did. I told him I wanted fifty dollars in gold for it. That was as much as two Colt revolvers were going for at the time, and I remember how his eyes looked when I told him the price. But he didn't say anything else, and for a while I thought the subject was closed for good.

Then one day about three weeks later, Scrappy Jack showed up at our cabin asking to see me. "I've got your cash." was all he said. Indeed, he was holding a California fifty dollar gold piece in his hand. Now for those who have never seen one, a California fifty dollar coin is the most beautiful sight in the world. It's so much bigger than our standard twenty dollar piece that it puts the smaller coin to shame. I've even seen people pay a premium, just to get a fifty for themselves. More than just money, the coin tends to break down resistance from reluctant sellers. I know it sure got to me!

I accepted the coin and the Quackenbush became his. With it went several boxes of cat slugs and more boxes of lead bullets. In all, he was outfitted to shoot for many years without a worry.

That was the last time I saw Scrappy Jack alive. He left our community and passed into legend, or so I thought.

With my newfound wealth, I went up to San Francisco and inquired by telegram of the Quackenbush factory how much a replacement gun would cost. Shipped from Herkimer to the west coast, it was $13.65, with 1,000 rounds of ammunition. Since I was flush, I bought two—one to use and the other to sell if another Scrappy Jack came my way. Two months later, my rifles arrived at the Union Pacific depot, and, before the week was out, they were both sold at a good profit.

The next time, I put all my money together, plus some my father had, and ordered ten guns from Quackenbush. They arrived in less than a month, together with a letter from the company asking if I would like to be a dealer. I had some time to think about it, as the new lot took more than a month to sell. It seemed to me I might improve my lot in life by selling them, so I applied to become a dealer. I also purchased guns from Daisy who advertised in one of the trade journals.

Within the year, I was selling so many guns that I was starting to have problems keeping up my end of the orchard. My father understood and bought out my share and I went into the gun and sporting-goods business full time. By the middle nineties, I was also stocking firearms from Colt, Smith & Wesson, Winchester, Remington and Marlin. The BB gun trade died off around the turn of the century and I converted to strictly a firearms store with a full-time gunsmith on the premises. Sales were brisk, as California was a sportsman's paradise, as well as a frontier territory.

One day, a man came in to buy a Colt pistol and asked if we took in guns as trades. I said we did and asked to see what he had. To my great surprise, he pulled my old Quackenbush out of a canvas bag. It was the worse for wear after all those years, but there was no doubt in my mind that this was indeed my old gun. I accepted it gladly and even gave a little more than the fellow expected, just to get my gun back again, for in a way, it was responsible for the business I was now in.

When I asked the man how he came by the gun, he shuddered and told me a dark tale. He found it in a small cave up in the hills above the community of Los Gatos. He said there were other things up there that he didn't want to talk about, but I made him draw me a map of the place just the same.

The next week, I set out on my horse to locate the spot on the map.

After two days of looking, I was sure I had found it. That was confirmed by the appearance of a semi-clothed skeleton tucked under some rocks, which I assumed was the small cave the man described. There wasn't much left, but somehow I knew that this was the body of Scrappy Jack, who had left thirteen years before.

I dug him a proper grave, although not as deep as one in a cemetery, and I dragged what was left of him into it. Saying a few words over the resting place of what I imagine could be considered a friend seemed strange, as it brought to my attention how little I really knew about the man. Then I remembered his stories about his "bank."

He said it was located in a grove of large trees, so nobody could spy on him when he was digging it up. But that was all he ever said about it. So I spent the rest of the time looking around for a grove of trees that fit the description. I didn't find them, but I did find the remnants of another more permanent camp with a lean-to that was still partially standing. Exploring this structure, I found two of the Quackenbush cat slugs laying in a corner. No doubt this was a place Scrappy Jack had holed up. Vowing to return, I rode back home.

I was able to get away again three months later, and rode straight to the old camp, to continue the search. I had recalled that Scrappy Jack had once mentioned the beautiful view from the place where his bank was located, and since the lean-to was not in such a place, I decided to look in a spot closer to the coast.

Two days later, I found another important clue. There was a rock that looked like an arrow pointing toward the coast, and I remembered Jack mentioning something about following the arrow when he went to his bank. I looked for three more days but found nothing. Then, as I was leaving, I looked at the arrow once more. It was pointing towards the coast, but it was also pointing towards a spot on the neighboring hill where there was a stand of low trees. From the look of the place, it might have been possible to see all the way to the coast from there.

I resolved to stay another day and explore the trees, as this was the best clue I had found thus far. It took half the day just to get my horse up on the hill where the trees were, and I had to backtrack once to be sure they were the right ones. When I got there, I immediately found a very suspicious looking grove of trees that looked just like the one Jack described.

The ground inside the grove was bare of grass because the closeness of the trees admitted little light. I allowed my eyes to adjust to the low light, then began to look for signs of disturbed earth. If Jack had been there within the past ten years, I figured there would be some signs. Indeed, there were!

I found a shallow depression in the ground almost in the center of the grove. There were old signs of a campfire there, but I was more intrigued by the way the ground dipped down in a shallow depression. From my days working in the orchard, I knew that the soil in this region never went back to its normal level, once disturbed. It always left a depression.

I started digging and within the first three feet my shovel hit something hard. Going slower, I uncovered the corner of an earthenware crock. Working quickly, I dug up the crock and found the surprise of my life. In two burlap sacks inside the crock were many hundreds of fifty dollar gold pieces, just like the one Jack had given me!

But the treasure didn't end there. Under the spot where crock number one had rested, were crocks two and three. Both were filled with sacks of the same contents as the first, but these held even more! It looked as though Jack had been digging up crock one only, because the other two were quite full.

I had to construct a travois for my horse to carry the coins back to my home because they were so heavy. Once there, I had to plan my next move. The money I now had in my possession was more than I would be able to make in a lifetime, but I couldn't just come out with it or people would want to know all the details.

Even in those early days, certain kinds of people were always trying to find out your private business. As soon as they found out where I got the wealth, there would come a flood of claimants, each with a convincing story of how the money was really theirs. The courts would listen to each of these thieves and enjoin me to not spend one cent of the money until the whole mess could be resolved. No sir, I did not want anyone to know where this gold had come from, or, indeed, that I had it at all!

But gold you can't spend is gold you don't have, in my book. So, here I was, a man with a fortune who was as poor as the next fellow because, if I spent a cent of it, I risked loosing it all! What a dilemma.

Then it occurred to me to do the very thing others had done—move out of there and change my identity. In a new locale, I could invent whomever I wanted to be and live however I desired. I resolved to pick a place where wealth would be easy to hide, but not so expensive that I couldn't afford to live there. The California climate had gotten into my blood by then, so I wanted to remain on the coast if possible.

In those days, the village of Los Angeles was growing rapidly. If I moved down there I would be far enough from the busybodies and yet still enjoy the beautiful California climate. So I sold the business in San Francisco to my gunsmith and got my things together to move. I was able to hire a train car to move me to my new home that had been selected for its seclusion. I was located on a rural street from which you could see the sun set every evening, tucked up against the hills overlooking the village of Los Angeles.

I spent many years in that house, until the booming movie industry had built up the town of Hollywood all around me. When I finally sold my five acre place, the profit netted me almost as much as the gold I originally found. Once again I had to move, but this time, there was no pressure to hide who I was.

In 1929, I attended the funeral of the famous Wyatt Earp, whose exploits made him the most well known figure of that time. Shortly afterward I sold my house in Hollywood and moved for what has proved to be the final time.

I'm now ensconced in a beautiful setting overlooking one of God's finest creations, beautiful Lake Tahoe, high up in the Sierra Nevada range. I was able to buy ten acres of property right on the lake, half of which lies in California and the other half in Nevada. The summers are hot and beautiful, while the winters are legendary! My home is remote enough to discourage casual visitors, yet close enough to Carson City that I can go to town if I want. The train is the only regular passage in and out of the mountains, most automobiles being too frail to make the trip reliably. The roads are primitive, which keeps the traffic to a minimum.

With the end of the war in sight, I can't wait to get out of my hideaway and travel to all the places we read about in the newspapers. I imagine I should allow a year or two for them to rebuild most of Europe, but England might still be nice. Oh well, I shall see.

My old Quackenbush air rifle is mounted on a polished walnut board in a place of honor over the mantle in my den, Each day, I read my newspaper and look out over the beautiful lake under the shadow of the small gun that brought so much happiness into my life. I often wonder what might have become of the gun that was made immediately after mine. Did it travel as widely and pass through as many hands, or was it owned by just one person who kept it in the closet all his life?

South shore of Lake Tahoe, on the state line
August 29, 1944

Chapter 6
Never let her down

Dennis Cathcart was my best friend when I was a kid. We used to play together every day, and we even managed to get assigned to the same class in school. If I did something, he did it too. If he was somewhere, I wasn't far behind. The two of us were as inseparable as two young boys can be and still have identities of their own.

One thing we both liked to do was play soldier. The war with Spain had just been fought, so there was a lot of military paraphernalia around, and two clever boys soon acquired quite a set of equipment for themselves. Dennis' mother was a great seamstress, so she sewed up uniforms for both of us. My mother didn't sew, but she was frequently the designated chuck wagon for the terrible twosome, because we tended to play at my house more often.

One day, my dad came home from work with an old BB gun someone had given him. They knew he had a boy and thought I might like to have a toy gun to play with. Since it was broken, both my parents thought I couldn't get into any trouble with it, although it still looked like a gun and had a lot of play value left in it.

Well, I was sure glad to get that gun, I can tell you! Until then I had never had a toy gun of any kind, because my mother was dead set against them. My father had an old shotgun he kept up in the attic, but he wasn't much of a shooter, and I never saw him use it.

Mother used to preach against little boys having guns because she said they always led to no good. I never thought she would let me keep this one, only when she saw how excited I was, I think she softened a little. I had to promise to never point it at anyone or at any animals, a promise I made without reservation.

When I showed the gun to Dennis, he was as excited as I was. His folks didn't have anything against guns; they just didn't happen to have a BB gun. We were both so young that the question of gun ownership was still several years away, and for me it would be even longer.

The first thing Dennis did was examine the new/old gun thoroughly.

It didn't have a trigger, so it wouldn't stay cocked, but the spring seemed quite strong. It was the kind of gun you cocked by pushing down the stock and sort of breaking the gun in the middle.

He then poured some oil down the barrel because his dad had told him BB guns ran on oil. Nothing happened, of course, but we both felt we were a step closer to having a working gun.

For the next several weeks that gun was our constant companion, going out into the field on military maneuvers and fighting marauding bandits and Indians. As we played with it, its stature grew in our minds, until there was nothing that gun could not do. It was perfectly accurate, unbelievably powerful and never out of ammunition. It kicked like a mule when it fired, but both Dennis and I were such hardy sportsmen that we never took notice. And we were certain that if the gun could ever be repaired, it would fulfill our wildest dreams.

Dennis' father looked at the gun one day and decided it could be fixed rather easily. All it took was a few small parts that he thought were easy to make. He was a handy guy who was always fixing something out in his garage, so this shouldn't have surprised me.

I had reservations about letting him fix the gun, though, for a couple of reasons. First, I wasn't as sure of his gunsmithing skills as he was. What if he tore it apart and couldn't get it back together again? Then I wouldn't even have a toy anymore. But worse than that, I think, was the possibility that he could fix it, which would leave me with a working gun. My mother would never go for that. If it worked, I could lose it forever.

Still, it's hard for a kid of seven to have a conversation like that with an adult. It seems strange after all these years that I was as astutely aware of the politics of the situation at seven, but believe me—I was!

So, Mr. Cathcart tore into the gun one Saturday, and, after three hours of work, he proved as good as his word. The gun was repaired and shooting. Dennis and I watched him the entire time, fascinated by the ingenuity he employed to get the job done. With just a few pieces of heavy wire and a small spring he found in his garage, he made the repair like a real gunsmith.

The moment of truth came when he was finished. The gun was ready to shoot. Since we didn't have any BB shot lying around, the three of us walked to the hardware store to buy some. They sold it in small paper tubes for a nickel, I think, and Mr. Cathcart treated us to the first tube.

Once we had the shot, there was no delaying the moment of truth. Mr. Cathcart let me fire the first shot because the gun was mine. I had been practicing for this moment for so many weeks that I was fully prepared for that shot, although the feel of a working trigger was a little strange.

We had been pretending that the back of the trigger guard was the trigger when the gun didn't work, and of course the new trigger was in a different position. The real trigger pull was very hard, but it broke cleanly and I managed to hit a jar lid about 15 feet away with the very first shot. Dennis had oiled the gun so well that the power was fully restored, so when we examined the lid, we found the shot had dented it deeply and even cracked the metal at the bottom of the dent. I was in seventh heaven! Now I had a real gun and it shot like a dream.

Dennis did well on his first shot, too, and Mr. Cathcart was as surprised as we were at the accuracy of the thing. I think we shot almost that entire tube of BB shot that day. The sun was low in the trees when I returned home.

Now I had a real dilemma. The "toy" gun wasn't a toy any longer. It was real. And it was powerful; I had seen that while shooting. Of course it was quiet, too. Not the loud rifle we imagined when we were just pretending. The recoil was pretty tame as well. If I was crafty about it, I could have probably pretended that the gun didn't work and no one would have been the wiser. I knew I would be safe with it—not getting in the BB gun wars that my mother feared so much. But she had only let me keep the thing because she thought it didn't work.

As much as she was opposed to guns, I was lucky just to have it. She didn't approve of guns in any way. So the future of my gun was up to me. I could lie and keep it or tell the truth and lose the best thing I ever had. At the tender age of seven, a fellow really doesn't know how many more good things there will be, so the tendency is to hang onto whatever you have as long as possible.

I even thought about asking Mr. Cathcart to take the parts out and make it into a toy again, but after that day's shooting I just couldn't bring myself to do it. I loved the way it shot so hard and straight that rendering it inoperable once again would have been like putting a pet to sleep.

I went to bed early that evening, worrying about my problem. I felt like a liar just having a working gun in my room when I knew so well how my mother felt about them. But I also wanted to keep it, because I had grown so attached to it. I tossed and turned all night long, wrestling with my problem.

The next morning was Sunday, and we went to church as always. In Sunday school, they taught us about how Solomon was so wise that he devised a clever way of determining which woman was the real mother of a child claimed by two women. The true mother was willing to give up the baby before seeing it cut in half, which was Solomon's way of bringing out her true love. He probably wouldn't have cut up that baby, although you never could tell about those Old Testament people. They were always cutting off thumbs and stuff like that, so maybe the mother was right to be afraid.

Anyhow—I figured that that was how I felt about my gun. I loved having it, but I loved the gun even more and didn't want to see it destroyed. I figured that if it went to Dennis, I would still be able to visit it and shoot it sometimes. So that afternoon, I told my mother what had happened and that I wanted to give Dennis the gun.

As I was telling her, tears started flowing from her eyes. I wish she hadn't done that, because soon I was crying right alongside of her. I figured she was sad because of the pain she was causing me by giving my gun away. I was sad for the same reason, but I never intended to start blubbering about it.

Then, she told me what was happening. She knew all about the gun being fixed. Mr. Cathcart had told her in church that day. She was waiting for me to tell her, to see what kind of citizen I was. Apparently, she knew what a rough time I was having over the decision. She had picked up on that the evening before.

To my surprise, she said I could keep the gun! Mr. Cathcart had told my dad how to take the trigger parts out so it wouldn't shoot, and they could put them back in when I was old enough for them. So that was what we did. The parts came out and went into a small vase in the living room and I got to play with the gun just like before. If I wanted to shoot it, I had to ask my mother or dad to put the parts back in, and they would supervise me while I shot. And that is how the strangest thing of all happened.

One day I asked my mother when my dad was coming home, because I wanted to shoot my gun. She said he wasn't coming home that day, because he was off to some volunteer firefighter camp for three days. I thought about asking whether Mr. Cathcart could do it, but before I asked, she told me he was at the same camp. But my mother said she would watch me shoot after she finished he laundry. So, to her complete surprise, I pitched in and helped her do it. Me—the kid who had to be reminded to put his clean socks away after they had been washed, dried and delivered to my bedroom was helping do the laundry without being asked!

We finished in short order, and then went out back to the shooting range my dad had fixed for me. We had done this before, but she had always just watched from a chaise lounge. This time she said she wanted to learn to shoot. Now it was my turn to be amazed. My gun-hating mother wanted to learn how to shoot!

Well, I figured this was my one chance to convert her to my thinking. I knew she was afraid of guns, so I told her everything there was to shooting the gun before she picked it up. Then, I had her watch me do it one time. When it was her turn, I watched her like a hawk.

Once, she turned around with the gun cocked and loaded, and I grabbed the barrel and pointed it towards the targets, the way my dad and Mr. Cathcart had taught me. They said to never point the barrel at something I didn't want to shoot, so that was what I told my mom. Me, a seven year-old kid was telling his own mother how to behave. But I knew I had to make her follow the rules, because if we had an accident I would probably never be allowed to shoot that gun again.

We shot for a long time that day, and when we were done, she handed the gun back to me and told me to get ready for supper. I reminded her that she needed to remove the trigger parts, but she said it was okay. I could keep them in from now on. I was flabbergasted!

At supper, she told me a story about when she was a little girl. It seems she had been tormented by a neighbor boy who shot at her with his BB gun. One time, he hit her cat, who had to be taken to the vet to have the shot removed. Ever since that time, she was dead set against guns of any kind, and especially BB guns. But she said I had shown her that not everybody had to act like that boy.

49

She was proud of the way I told her the truth about the gun working again, but even prouder that I acted responsibly when we were shooting together that afternoon. She said she now knew she could trust me to act responsibly with my gun, so from then on it was mine to shoot.

My mother never really got over her hatred of guns. I would love to report that she became an avid shooter and so on, but it didn't happen. But she did trust me to act in a responsible manner, which kept me even more vigilant than I would normally have been. Even when I got to be an old man, I still thought about her whenever I picked up a gun of any kind. I am happy to report that I never let her down.

Franklin Township, New Jersey 1948

Chapter 7
How I bought my BB gun

You're looking at the first real joy of my life and the last thing that never gave me a moment's disappointment. The thing I remember most about my BB gun was the effort it took to acquire. It wasn't given to me as a gift. I had to earn it, and that was at a time when kids were expected to do a lot of work for free. My chores were enough to keep me occupied for several hours each day, and because they didn't all happen at the same time, I was always hopping on to another household task.

Don't misunderstand; there was plenty of free time when I was growing up. Especially in the summer. But chores came first, and nobody ever thought much of it—we just did what was expected of us. So the time available to make money was somewhat limited, and there was almost no way to make money at home, the way children do nowadays. To make money, you had to find a job away from home that no adult wanted to do, and you had to do it for very little money.

You might think just because BB guns cost a dollar or two that we could buy one in a week. Let me tell you, in the 1890s, a nickel bought a whole ice cream sundae, and a dime could buy you a lunch. Shoeshines went for a nickle, and Detroit was so full of shoeshine boys that there was no money in it for a kid starting out. What you needed was an angle. Something that nobody else had thought of and also something that people would pay good money for. Not much different than today, is it?

In the winter you could shovel sidewalks, but the money you made from that was spent in no time. I was expected to pay my own way for things like candy, soda pop and other childhood treats. A ticket to the carnival was bought by my parents, but they went along, too. There was no way to cage anything from that.

Other kids were no source of money. They were all just as poor as I was. No—whatever scheme I hit on had to be attractive to adults, and they had to be willing to pay real money for it. I daydreamed that I found something that paid me a dime and that hundreds of people lined up for it. I never concentrated on what it was—just the fact that there was money and it was coming to me. What actually happened, though, was much stranger than anything I had imagined.

Near my home was a lake that people flocked to in the summer for swimming and boating. I went there because it didn't cost anything, and I loved to swim. In fact, that was how I found out how to get real money faster than any kid had ever dreamed.

Out in the lake there was a diving platform that pretty much belonged to the older boys. If you were a kid like me and you tried to climb up on the platform, some older boy would probably throw you off again. We learned not to tempt fate by going out there in the middle of the day.

The boys did all kinds of crazy antics to impress the girls who came to the lake. At any time of the day, there would be boys doing handstands or headstands on the platform, or else belly-flopping to see who could make the biggest splash. These boys were in their late teens, and many of them had summer jobs that paid real money. Sometimes, one of them would catch a girl's eye and he would swim in to buy her a lemonade or something from the concession stand, until her mother called her away. It went on all day every day, and everybody just accepted it.

One day I happened to hear a boy tell his friend that he had lost two quarters from his swimsuit. There were pockets with buttons in them in those old-style swimsuits, but if you weren't careful, things could fall out. He said they had fallen out while he was doing a handstand on the platform, and that started my head to spinning. If he had lost money that way, I wondered how many other boys had lost some, too?

That evening, I asked my father just how long the swimming lake had been there. He said he went to it when he was a little boy back in the '70s, so he supposed it was older than that. I then asked him if the diving platform had been there, too, and he smiled and asked whether I had ever been thrown off. He said the platform was the same one he had played on as a kid, except they had rebuilt it a few years back when the boards rotted out. That was when I got my idea.

If the platform had been there all those years and if boys had been doing the same crazy things all that time, there must be a bundle of money at the bottom of the lake. All someone had to do was go down and get it. At least that's how it seemed to me when I went to bed that evening.

The next day I went over to the lake, but there was no way to try out my idea because boys were diving off the platform constantly all day long. If they saw me bring up money from the bottom, the jig would have been up and I wouldn't have been able to go near there. So I had to do it all in secret.

The following morning, I went to the lake at 6 a.m., a full three hours before it opened to the public. I had my bathing suit on under my clothes, and I changed in the bushes. I had to sneak into the lake because the caretaker would have pitched me out on my ear if he had caught me. In the cold water, I swam out to the platform, where it first dawned on me—I didn't know how deep the water was. What if it was a hundred feet? The only way to find out was to dive as deep as I could and to try and feel for it.

I was a good swimmer, but on the first dive, I ran out of air before I felt the bottom. Second dive, too. On the third dive, I tried to see the bottom, but the lake was murky and I saw nothing. On the fifth and final dive, I saw a piece of board that must have been sticking up from the bottom. That gave me some hope that I would be able to reach it eventually. But not this day. I was too tired and cold to continue, so I snuck out of the water, got my clothes and went home.

The rest of my free time that day, I sat in the parlor, practicing holding my breath while watching the second hand of our clock. In the beginning, I couldn't hold it longer than 45 seconds, but after some practice, I was up to a minute and twenty seconds. By the end of the day, I held my breath a minute and thirty-eight seconds, which was more than twice as long as the first time.

For the next several days, I worked on my breath holding until I had cracked two minutes thirty seconds. I learned to take several deep cleansing breaths before trying to hold one, and this really improved my time.

The next time I went to the lake in the morning, I was much better prepared. I had cooking grease to rub on my arms and legs to make the cold less chilling, and I was able to stay down a reasonable length of time. This time, I reached the bottom of the lake, which was between twelve and fifteen feet at that spot. It was cold and dark, but I was now where I wanted to be.

The bottom was all clay mud and very slick to the touch. I hated putting my hands on it, until finally I felt a coin. My first coin, and it felt like quarter! I rose quickly to the surface to clean it off, and sure enough, it was a shiny new quarter. I was finally on my way to financial freedom and BB gun ownership.

That day, I found two more quarters and a penny, so the total was seventy-six cents. That was already enough to buy a cheap BB gun, but that wasn't what I was after. I wanted the best, and now that I knew how to find money for free, I would have it!

The next time I went back I didn't find anything except a cheap brass ring someone had lost. I kept it, even though it brought me no closer to my goal. What I needed was a way to go through more of the ooze on the bottom, and to bring whatever I found to the surface to look at it. I thought about that problem all the next day with no great insights, until my mother asked me to go to the store. She needed a dozen eggs, a sack of flour and some butter.

At the store, I watched the clerk scoop the flour out of a big barrel and put it into a small cloth sack that he tied shut. It was the same kind of sack I now carried to put my diving finds in. If only I could scoop the mud up from the bottom the way the clerk scooped out the flour. Then it hit me. Why couldn't I? Why couldn't I do exactly that and spend less time on the bottom, but bring up more stuff?

I raced home with mother's items and then asked if I could go over to the dump. She didn't like me going there because the place was dirty and I always brought home neat stuff, but she said if I finished mowing the yard, I could go. I tell you, grass has never been cut so fast as ours was that afternoon. Then it was off to the dump to make my money scoop.

I settled on a large tin can with the edges beaten down so they wouldn't cut me. I hammered nails through the can to make holes for the water and muck to drain, and those had to be beaten flat on the inside, too. After about an hour, my money scoop was finished.

The next morning, I hurried over to the lake to try out my new invention. Let me tell you—it worked on the very first try! After sifting through all the mud in the can, I found fifty-six cents! It took about five times as long to make one dive and sort through the can, but I used the extra time in between dives to breathe deeply for the next dive. I found a dollar and fifty-three cents on the very next dive!

I already had my BB gun, plus money left over for BB shot. My third dive netted me forty-seven cents and a real gold ring! I was beside myself with joy. Surely I had discovered the way to a fortune by simply diving for it. One more dive brought up only twelve cents, but it also almost got me caught, too. The caretaker was now out and walking the beach, looking down at the sand for something. I swam quietly to the other side of the platform and waited for him to move on before I snuck back out of the water.

Hurrying home, I was mentally adding up my finds when the

thought struck me, how would I explain my newfound wealth to my parents? They would want to know where I had gotten the money, and I didn't want to tell them, for they were certain to disapprove.

Even if they let me keep it, they would insist that at least half be deposited in my savings bank, which was a cast iron box I kept beside my bed. Father had the key to that box and the rule was, half of whatever I made had to go in the bank. Twice a year, my father took out the contents and deposited them in a real bank downtown for me. I probably had lots of money down there, but it wasn't of much use to me.

After beating the hall runners for my mother, I went back over to the lake to think about my situation. I was sitting on a bench when the old caretaker walked up and sat down beside me. He asked how I was and how my summer had been going, and I said something, I suppose. Then, he surprised me by telling me he had seen me sneaking out of the lake several times in the past few mornings. He said he was wondering what I was up to, but he thought he had figured it out this morning. He said he figured I was diving for something I lost out by the platform.

I was trying to think of a good excuse to tell him when he shared a secret with me. He said that he walked along the beach every morning to look for valuables and money people lost. That must have been what he was doing when I saw him earlier that day.

I decided to tell him what I was doing because he had confided in me, so I did. I told him the whole story, including the part about wanting a great BB gun. He said he would help me. He said he would tell my folks I was working for him doing some cleanup jobs, and I could then tell them that the money came from that. Half would still have to go in the bank, but at least I would be able to use the other half. It meant that I was now just over halfway to my goal, but I figured I could get the rest in a few more mornings.

The next morning, I showed up bright and early, and Mr. Carpenter was there to greet me. This time I didn't have to sneak around in the bushes taking off my clothes. I swam out to the platform and began diving. But this morning, for some reason, all I found was twelve cents. I would never get my gun at that rate.

When I showed Mr. Carpenter my meager finds, he asked where I was diving and I told him. He said he thought the best place to check might be about twenty feet to the left, because that was where the first diving platform had been. When they rebuilt it, they moved it to a deeper place. Because it was getting late in the morning and I didn't want my secret to be discovered, I left the lake, but the next morning I was back, ready to try the new place.

On the first dive, I found that the bottom was less than ten feet deep, so I could really scoop up some mud. I brought up a whole can full and sloshed it around at the surface. To my amazement, there was a dollar and ninety-five cents in that load, plus something else I wasn't quite sure of. It was round and coppery looking, so I dropped it into the sack tied on my waist and continued diving. That day, I brought up a total of six dollars and seventy-seven cents. And, when I got back to the shore, I looked at the other thing I had found and it turned out to be a 2-1/2 dollar gold coin! That pushed my total for the day to over nine dollars! I was ecstatic, but of course I couldn't tell my folks that Mr. Carpenter was paying me that kind of money. That was almost what my father made in a week!

I returned to the lake many more times that summer and eventually pulled out sixty-five dollars in good cash money. Besides that, I found three gold rings, fourteen silver ones, nine religious medals on chains, one gold anklet with a name on it and a set of false teeth!

I brought home a much smaller amount of cash on a weekly basis, and eventually had enough extra saved up to buy my Daisy. Once I got it, what remained of the summer was spent in the fields and vacant lots rather than in the water. I still went back, and the finds continued to come in, but the initial thrill had long since worn off. The extra money I hid and only dipped into sparingly, so nobody would notice. It lasted several years.

The next year, the lake was put under stricter town management, and my deal with Mr. Carpenter was over. They put up a high fence around the beach, which made getting in to dive very difficult. I still went there during the day, and I even managed a few "hands-only" dives on my secret hot spot, but the days of bringing up real money were over.

Still, every time I looked at my Daisy, I couldn't help remembering all I had to do to get it. I never told that story before now, because even as an adult I was afraid of what my parents might have thought. I kept that gun throughout my youth and into adulthood. We sort of grew up and old together. Today it needs a little more oil than it used to and the shots are not as powerful as they once were, but I can say the same things about myself. But even in my old age, I can still hold my breath longer than three minutes, and I sometimes dream of diving for treasure again.

Chapter 8
Long time coming

That wasn't my gun I was holding. The photographer told me to hold it, over the protests of my mother who wanted me to just stand there at attention. He convinced her that it would make me look more like a little man if I held a gun and stood in a casual pose like that. He even took the shots my mother wanted and did this one at the end, saying she didn't have to pay for it if she didn't like how it turned out. As it happened, both she and my dad liked it best of all, and the others were never purchased, as far as I know.

I was not allowed to have a gun like that because my mother didn't want me growing up to fight in a war like her brother had. He was killed in Cuba before we got the upper hand in that war, and my mother never got over it. She told me I should never touch a gun or even look at one because that was how her brother lost his life.

Her feelings were strong enough that my father never brought up the subject in our house. I think he had been something of a hunter in his younger years, because my uncles told me about some of his exploits in the field, but I couldn't get a word about it from him.

Now, all my boy cousins had guns. So, whenever we went visiting, I got to sneak in some furtive time examining them. My one cousin, Bobby, even let me shoot his BB gun when I slept over at his house. It had to be done on the sly, you understand, because Bobby's parents knew how my mother felt and would never have sanctioned my shooting if they had known.

BB guns were not that common when I was a boy, so my friends didn't have them as young boys often do today. Some had their own .22s that their fathers would take them out to shoot from time to time, but that was controlled by the parents, and I was never invited, even to watch.

As you might imagine, all of this denial and deprivation built up a tremendous curiosity about guns and a desire to own and shoot them. It became the central theme in my life. Of course when you're young you think your parents run the world, but as you begin to grow up you realize they don't and that some day things will start going your way.

For me, that day came when I was shipped off to preparatory school. There had been talk of military school before that, but my father put his foot down and refused to consider it. But preparatory school was common for families where the kids were expected to attend college.

My prep school was located in Massachusetts, in the hills overlooking Boston. It was supposed to be one of the top prep schools for Harvard, which is why I got to go, but what my mother never knew was that it was also allied with the most famous America rifle range of all—Walnut Hill.

By the time I got there, the range had been in operation for a long, long time. Some of the most famous offhand matches had been shot there, and the list of names of those who had graced the grounds was legendary. Even with her prejudice against guns, my mother had no doubt heard of the likes of Captain Hill, G.H. Wentworth, Mr. W. Lowe, Charles Hinman, Ross, and the great Harry Pope! They were the stars of the day, as famous as heavyweight prize-fighters and baseball players have become today. Their names were in all the prominent newspapers; indeed, the Boston Globe was one of their strongest backers and even fielded a team of women sharpshooters. Quite a progressive notion for the early part of this century.

As a student, I was offered a job pulling targets in the pits at Walnut Hill, which I accepted, of course. Through the low offices of that position, I met and associated with some of America's finest shooters, as well as no limit of local gun cranks who also used the facility. Doctors, lawyers, and bankers were all a part of the great American pageant of rifle shooting at that time, and Walnut Hill became the place where they met to socialize and to conduct their business, as well.

In time, I was adopted in spirit by several wealthy gentlemen and my association with firearms began in earnest. They loaned me their second guns with the equipment I needed to make bullets and to load them. I bought the powder and primers from my earnings in the pits, and the lead was free for the taking—one of the advantages of being in the pits. I even cast lead pigs from some of the surplus and sold it to the members to get money for more powder and primers.

The year I was accepted to Harvard, I was already in solid with the group at Walnut Hill and could return at any time to shoot with them. At college, I joined the rifle team, where I was afforded the opportunity to continue my surreptitious avocation without a break. My studies were in finance, but my time at the range proved to be as valuable as any three classes, from the contacts and associations I made.

After school I accepted a position with a Boston bank, where I was in the department that handles trusts. Through my connections at Walnut Hill, I quickly came to the attention of the Managing Director, who, though not a shooter himself, recognized that his clients all knew me by my first name and were most willing to see me professionally, despite my youth.

About that time, my mother discovered the double life I'd been leading. She and my dad were attempting to transfer some of their finances to my bank as a show of support when someone blurted out that I was the talk of the Walnut Hill crowd. This distressed her greatly. So much so that the transfer never happened, I'm afraid. For several months I was persona non grata at home, where I fortunately no longer resided.

I was never forgiven my indiscretion, but things were patched back up on the surface, so I could return home at holidays and for short visits. Meanwhile, my success at the bank continued right up to the market crash in 1929, where so many investors were wiped out. Although my bank fared better than most, the depression was so universal that it soon locked up all commerce regardless of who had money. In fact, in those days it wasn't safe to let folks know you had money, so we all just hunkered down and tried to wait it out.

But the depression finished off Walnut Hill for me. The Great War had tainted everything that had a German name attached to it, and of course our shooting was fairly riddled with them, so it became unpopular to talk about it in polite company. Then the depression took away most of the wealth, and the thing finally died on its own. Oh, the ranges were still there and you would see a few cranks out there from time to time, but gentlemen seemed to forget the halcyon days of the Election Day matches and the great shooters of the past. Fine offhand rifles by Schalk and Pope were bored out and remodeled into varmint rifles shooting bullets at 3,000 feet per second, and nobody wanted to shoot just one shot at a time at targets any more.

I retired after the Second World War and settled down to a life of relative leisure for the first time in my life, except it wasn't a life I really wanted to live. The luster and grandness remembered from my youth had been replaced by the hustle and bustle of a world trying to rebuild itself again. There was little room for a man who wanted to spend a day at the range shooting a front-loading single shot cartridge target rifle. I could find no one to talk to who recalled the same glorious days I did. I was very lonely.

Then one day my mother passed away and I inherited her house and furnishings. It took several weeks to sort through the items I wanted to keep, and that's when this picture was discovered again. It had hung in our parlor for many years, but after our great rift over Walnut Hill, it was consigned to a musty trunk in the attic.

When I saw myself holding that little Quackenbush again, all the desires and longings of my youth poured over me in a flood. Only I realized that now I was of an age and had the means to do something about it. So I set about seeking and acquiring the airguns and BB guns that had been denied to me as a boy. I am quite sure my mother was turning over in her grave at my actions but the time had come for the little boy to get his wishes fulfilled.

Over the next 12 years I acquired a collection of American airguns that was unrivaled, as far as I knew. There were Quackenbushes, Daisys, Kings and Markhams, as well as a hundred other makes of airguns less well known, but just as desirable to me. I traveled to Philadelphia in search of robust Columbian guns; to upstate New York to find the gorgeous nickel-plated Quackenbushes; to Michigan to find the greatest assortment of BB gun brands ever made; to St. Louis to scout out both the St. Louis airguns and the plethora of Benjamins that followed; and to many other cities to look in junk stores, gun stores and antique shops. My card is on file with more than 200 antique dealers today. Although I am never exactly certain, my collection numbers something over 4,000 of the diminutive shooters.

Today, I spend my time playing with my guns as I should have at the turn of the century. Although I own single shot rifles by Pope that will put five bullets inside an inch at 200 yards on a good day, my greatest thrills are holding and shooting guns that can't do as well at 20 feet. That these little wonders can function at all using just plain air astonishes me, as does the genius that went into their construction.

Most of the airgun manufacturers are now gone, as are many of the people who actually made the guns. There has never been a book about any one of them, to my knowledge, so I have to fill my thirst by owning and admiring the guns, themselves.

Perhaps someday people will realize that nothing man makes is either good or bad. The thing is not what makes the good or the bad, it is the intent of the person using it. I lost a childhood from the mistaken belief that all guns are bad, and that, by not associating with them, one can be cleansed from the desire to shoot. In fact, that attitude is probably what gave force to the all-consuming desire I have today. If you are ever a parent or in a position of influence over a child, you might consider my story before condemning an entire class of objects based on fear alone.

San Francisco, 1959

Chapter 9
Little Chief

You grow up as a kid thinking that the whole world is exactly the same. That all kids are just like you and every place is like the places you've seen. Slowly, this fantasy begins to break down as your experience grows. Sometimes the breakdown is painful; other times it's delightful and still other times it can be just plain strange.

When I was a boy in 1920, life was pretty good. Although I had no way of gauging things then, in retrospect I see that I was well provided for and very fortunate in selecting my parents. My mother was a former debutante and my father was a successful lawyer, who later entered politics. My maternal grandmother also lived with us for a long time, so I got to know her quite well, too. She ran an antique store in our town, which afforded me the opportunity of seeing the finest furnishings, housewares and art that were to be seen in a small Ohio town. After I matured to adulthood and had a family of my own, my taste in furnishings was impeccable as a result of this long association.

But there was another reason I enjoyed my grandmother's company. She was a gun enthusiast! Through her dealings in the trade, she came across scores of fine firearms, many of which she bought and sold through her store. And the prices were unbelievable. Often, when a man would die, grandmother would be called by the widow and asked to dispose of certain items of the estate. If the man kept guns, these would almost certainly be at the top of the list. Many of the widows would feign great fear and loathing for the evil thundersticks and would not even touch them. They wanted the house to be rid of their evil spirits, and the sooner the better.

My grandmother began teaching me about guns when she saw I had an interest at a very early age. My father couldn't be bothered with them, except that he did attend the local shooting matches on holidays, simply because that's where all his clients were. But at home, his interests ran to the garden and to his new automobiles. Guns were of no interest whatsoever, despite the fact that his only son was completely captivated by them.

But grandma made up for his lack in spades! Often, when there was nobody in the shop, she would let me hold some of her guns as she narrated their story. I got to see rare 18th century Kentucky long guns, European fowling pieces, fine Schuetzen rifles, military guns of long ago and one time she had a Winchester model 1873 marked "One of One Thousand!" She didn't have that gun long and I never found out what it sold for, but the day she sold it she took the whole family to a fine restaurant for a steak dinner with all the trimmings. That much I remember.

Another bit of fallout from her shop were the airguns that passed through. Since they looked like guns to the widows, they came along with the rest of the estate property. Grandma had a much harder time selling them, so I often got to play with them and even to keep them for a while. A good Daisy BB gun would fetch all of fifty cents or so, and we would wait a year or more for it to sell, so there was always a nice selection of BB guns for me to enjoy. Like I said, I had no idea at the time what a perfectly wonderful life I was enjoying.

As kids, we played lots of different games, but I suppose the best of them had to be cowboys and Indians. Almost every kid wanted to be a cowboy, with most claiming to be Wyatt Earp or Wild Bill Hickock. I, on the other hand, preferred to be an Indian for some reason. I suppose my grandmother's shop had something to do with the choice.

While we rarely had anything cowboy-related, we were in Ohio, which has a very rich Indian tradition. There were always lots of Indian artifacts in the store. I got to see arrowheads, moccasins, tobacco pouches, bows and arrows and sometimes even ceremonial dress items. I couldn't explain why these things fascinated me, but they did. Whenever I would go to the cinema and watch the cowboy reels, I knew the fights with the Indians were fake. If cowboys were such good fighters, why did General Custer get wiped out at the Little Big Horn? That was something my friends could never tell me.

71

I even had an Indian outfit that my mother made for me. It's the one in the picture. The clothes were made of real buckskin which my grandmother donated from her shop and the headdress was made of turkey feathers with the tips dyed black to look like eagle feathers. I was so proud of that outfit because I looked more like an Indian chief than any of my friends looked like the cowboys they were trying to be. At best all they had was an old fedora hat that someone had remodeled to look like a western Stetson.

When we played, we carried toy guns or BB guns, if we had them, although there was a strict rule that all BB guns had to be unloaded and never cocked. That rule was sanctioned by the mothers who would not hesitate to break up the game if they saw an infraction. Supposedly a kid had caught a BB in the cheek years before, which led to the strict enforcement of the rule.

One day while we were alone in the shop, I asked my grandmother about the Indians of Ohio. She always seemed to know a lot of history, and could tell you things that weren't to be found in any book. Well, this day, she told me something that I haven't told another soul in all my life! She told me I was part Indian!

That's right. I am one-sixteenth Indian. Here's how it happened. My grandmother was half French-Canadian by birth. Her grandmother had been pure Indian and her grandfather had been a French fur trapper, before Canada was even a country. That made my grandmother one-fourth Indian, which made my mother one-eighth and me one-sixteenth American Indian. I was thrilled at the thought.

My grandmother told me about the Algonquin tribe, which was a strange tribe of people, some of whom had blond hair and blue eyes. They mostly died off in the later 1700s from smallpox brought in by the European immigrants—especially the French, who intermarried with them. By 1920, there were no more pure-blooded Algonquins left, and it was rare to even find someone who had their blood. I wanted to know more, so she arranged a trip for us to Ohio State University. I got to see the museum where a large number of artifacts were stored.

A man in the museum told me a lot about the Algonquin tribe, and we found out later that he wrote books on the subject, but of course he didn't mention that to us. He wanted to know why a six-year-old boy was so interested in a lost tribe, but I had been sworn to secrecy by my grandmother, so I couldn't tell him the real reason. She had explained to me that other people viewed Indians differently than I did and that it wasn't a good idea to tell people that I was part Indian for fear of what people might think.

As a result, I carried the secret all my life, never telling anyone who and what I really was. When I entered the Marine Corps in World War II, I discovered that grandma had been right—people really did care about such things and they could make life very difficult for those who carried Indian blood in their veins. I met and even became friends with a full-blooded Pima Indian in the Corps. He had very few friends in the unit and was razzed constantly about being an Indian. He even looked like one. In contrast to my blond hair and fair skin, his skin was dark brown and stretched tight over his high cheekbones.

He and I served all the way through the Pacific, until I got hit on Iwo Jima and evacuated to a hospital ship. That was the end of the war for me, but my friend, who everybody called "Chief," went on to fight a few more days. Then President Truman requested that he be returned to the United States immediately.

You have probably seen him but don't know it. He is the last man in the famous photo and statue, "The flag-raising on Iwo Jima." His name is Ira Hayes. He's the man with outstretched arms who has just let go of the flagpole, raising the flag of the land he fought for—the same land that took his ancestral grounds and scattered his people to the four winds.

Ira died an alcoholic in 1954 at the age of 33, afflicted with that dreaded sickness that seems to plague the American Indian. I have the disease, myself, although I have never allowed it to manifest itself fully.

As I sit here in my comfortable home looking back over all the years, I think of Ira and of my grandmother who taught me so many things. My life will soon be over, but I have managed to touch the lives of others who will live on long past me. And I have finally discovered the secret to life on earth. It doesn't matter who you are or where you come from. What matters is how you behave and what you do with what you have. You are here long enough to have a small impact on mankind, then your turn is over and you are whisked away to the infinite.

My being part Indian did not affect my life one small iota, because I pretended that it wasn't true. I could get away with the lie because I didn't look like an Indian. Even though I admired the American Indian, I was too afraid I'd be embarrassed if anyone knew that I had their blood in me. Well, nobody ever knew.

Ira could not do the same. He lived the life he was given and became one of our country's most well-recognized heroes, even though most people never knew his name. They looked down on him both before and after his brave act, but he never stopped being himself. That's what makes a true hero. I wish now, as my life draws down to its final act, that I had possessed the bravery to be a real Indian.

Stow, Ohio, 1967

Chapter 10
By the book

If you asked me what kind of shooting I did as a kid, I would probably tell you that I didn't shoot a gun until I entered the Army. But this picture tells a different story. When I saw it again after all the years it brought back a flood of childhood memories I hadn't thought about for forty years and more. The first, and by far the most important recollection was of my grandmother's house, which is where this picture was taken.

My family lived in a small town in northern Indiana. It was a town that my father's people had settled more than 150 years before, but by the time I came along it was fully developed and the only recognition of our family was the large number of headstones that bore the same name in the cemetery. I had missed the golden age of our family by about 75 years, according to the dates on those graves.

I used to go to the graveyard often because it was so close to our house. In fact, us kids played in the vacant part of the cemetery much of the time because there was so much land that was open and flat. On summer nights we used to go over there to catch lightning bugs and tell ghost stories among the tombstones. We thought it was a neat place to be.

But my grandmother's house was the best of all. It was the one place where I could really let my hair down and do the things I wanted to do all the time, but was not permitted to. My own home was not so nice.

My mother was raising her family according to books she would get, and we had various restrictions imposed by the whim of authors whom we had never met. If someone wrote about the dangers of breathing the night air, all the windows in the house were locked shut at dusk—no matter how hot and stifling it was. If alfalfa pills were touted as being good for the liver, we took them every day. If cow's tongue was considered brain food, we ate it at least once a week. Whatever the writer was promoting, we followed along in perfect lockstep, never questioning the pedigree of the advice.

The funny thing was, a lot of the time one author would write something contrary to what another had said, and then we would go and do just the opposite thing that we had been doing, to comply with this newfound wisdom. My mother had no problem switching gears to the latest quack who obviously had the latest word. I can remember one day going from taking castor oil every day to seeing the bottle disposed of because it was thought to be a dangerous poison to young systems! I happened to agree with that view, by the way.

Well, as you might imagine, guns were never on any author's good list, at least not in the literature my mother subscribed to. She had testimonies from various women's groups and even from some milksop men, claiming that the association with guns was the first step to a life of crime. As a result, I wasn't allowed to have any guns as toys, nor was I allowed to associate with kids who did. If my mother caught one of my friends with so much as a cap gun in his possession, it was tantamount to disaster. The young miscreant was invited to go home immediately, while my mother got his mother on the phone and bent her ear for an hour on the horrors of guns in the hands of kids. I suppose she was the butt of many jokes for this, but of course adults never talk about such things openly in front of kids.

A funny thing I only learned much later in life was that many women's magazines, such as Cosmopolitan and, much later, Redbook, wholly supported kids learning how to use guns. They often spoke of teaching young boys to be "manly" men, something a mother was supposed to hope for, I guess. But my mother never read those articles, or if she did, their message went unheeded. Guns were evil in her eye, and she continued to convince herself even if it took the writings of characters with whom she would not normally associate.

But over at my grandmother's, there was a sanctuary waiting for me. All the accumulated flotsom and jetsom of eight healthy kids (six boys!) was tucked not-so-neatly into every nook and cranny of the basement, attic and garage of her huge Victorian house. There were things there that I never knew existed and have never seen others since. And there were the more mundane things—things a boy of 13 could relate to.

For one thing, and I thought it to be the most important thing, all of Grandma's boys had been shooters. Not just casual shooters—real dyed-in-the-wool get-up-at-four-in-the-morning-and-stay-out-till-dark shooters.

Their firearms weren't at her house, of course; they had taken them when they moved out, but the remnants were still visible. Shooting trophies, stuffed game animals, antique reloading tools and books on shooting abounded in that house. There were photographs of all the boys pursuing their favorite shooting sports. Some were of hunting scenes, but most were from the range, and were dated about thirty years earlier. I even found some pictures of my father, who had apparently been something of an offhand rifle shot in his day.

Then one day I found what I was looking for. I hadn't known that I had been looking for anything in particular, but when I found it I knew it was what I wanted all along. There, in a red felt bag, was an old Daisy BB gun! It had obviously seen better days, but it could still be cocked and I hoped that it shot as well.

I showed my find to my grandmother and she seemed to recall that the gun had belonged to one of my older uncles. "I doubt if he even remembers having it," she said. "Why don't you keep it?"

She must have known how much I wanted that old BB gun, it being one of the few real guns I had ever seen outside a picture. I knew absolutely nothing about how a gun worked, but Grandma did! She unscrewed the barrel—what I now know to be the shot tube—and dropped several drops of oil down the outer tube with the gun standing upright on its butt. "They need to be oiled a lot. Don't forget that, or it won't shoot hard for you."

From another box in the basement, she produced several tubes of lead BBs. She told me these were the kind the guns used to shoot before the war, and that my gun would only work well with them. "I don't think they still sell lead BB shot, but I have a friend who owns a gun store, so we'll find more for you when these run out. As I recall, the newer steel BBs are too small and hard to work well in these older guns. Plus, they bounce back pretty severely and have been known to put a boy's eye out."

That was the first time anyone had ever explained to me the universal fear all mothers seemed to have about BB guns putting out eyes. I had always thought everyone was afraid kids would intentionally shoot each other in the eyes with their guns, but that was not the case— or at least that's not how it got started. It seems that before the 1920s, all BB guns shot lead shot that didn't ricochet much at all. Then, in about 1925 or so, the BB guns makers began selling steel shot, and that's when the trouble began. A generation of boys used to using lead shot were suddenly getting maimed by the bounceback of the newer steel shot.

Nobody explained this to the public at the time, of course, and before long the mothers of America had banded together in a grass roots movement to keep the dangerous guns out of their son's hands. After another generation had passed, the phrase, "You'll shoot your eye out" was ingrained in everyone's mind, while the actual cause for it had faded into obscurity. In a single moment, my Grandmother had made all this crystal clear to me, as well as reinforcing the point that lead shot was all I should shoot in my new-old gun.

But the surprises were just beginning. Next, she took me over to another dusty corner where she got a stool to climb up to reach a box on top of some window frames. She brought it down and handed it to me, saying, "Go ahead—open it!"

Inside, I found a bow and four colorful arrows. It looked like a serious weapon, and Grandma said it had a 40 pound pull, but I could see that—it was written on the inside of the wood, just above the leather handle. She said, "Let's take it outside and see how you do."

We got a large cardboard box and filled it with newspapers, then leaned it against the base of a large tree in her back yard. She told me how to put the string on the bow, but she said I had to do it myself. She said that was the way to tell if I was big enough to use that bow. Well, don't you know I would have been able to string that bow if it had belonged to Hercules, himself, after a remark like that!

Then she talked me through the shooting routine. I was standing about 20 feet away from the box, and I hit it on the first try. Several more gave the same results. It seemed as though I was born to shoot a bow. Finally, she suggested we back up to about 40 feet, and I was still able to hit the box on every try. Somehow, I knew where the arrow was going before I let go of the bowstring. I can't explain it; I just knew.

Then I asked Grandma to try, and to my surprise, she welcomed the chance. Her first shot went through the box at the point in the center where all four flaps were folded over each other! Dead center!

When I asked her how she did it, she seemed embarrassed and muttered something I couldn't hear about practice. I later learned that most people practiced archery during the Victorian era when my Grandmother was younger, and that she had been something of a local champion.

We continued to shoot that afternoon, and I suppose she snapped that picture of me while we were at it. When the day was over she told me I could leave my BB gun and bow at her house and could use them whenever I came over. I was overjoyed because now I not only had the chance to shoot as much as I wanted, I even had a shooting partner in my Grandmother, who, as far as I was concerned, was my new best friend.

I went home that day refreshed, knowing that, from then on, my life was going to be much better, now that I had a safe haven to visit. I didn't know until then that there was even such a thing as pressure, but it was sure obvious when it went away! Life got better by a large amount.

The next morning at breakfast, however, everything changed in one moment. When I came down to breakfast, I could see that my mother had been crying and my father seemed very quiet, as well. After I ate, my dad took me into the living room and told me that Grandma Sims had passed away the evening before!

I couldn't believe it! She was dead? I had just been with her all the day before and nothing seemed wrong. In fact, she seemed in great health to me. Dad said it had been very sudden and unexpected. She simply collapsed at her dinner table and was pronounced dead when the doctor arrived. A neighbor had been sharing dinner with her and he called the ambulance, but her doctor got there first.

The funeral was held three days later. It was the first funeral I ever attended, and I really let myself go. I loved that woman so much! There was some kind of reception held at our house, but I stayed in my room and cried.

Over the next few days the family decided what to do with Grandma's place. All of the families got to take whatever they wanted from the house, but that didn't include my bow and BB gun, of course. I mentioned it to my dad and even tried to reason with him, but he knew how strongly my mother felt and he wasn't willing to go against her.

I was completely demoralized by the passing of my grandmother. Not only did it mean the loss of my most recently acquired prized possessions, it meant I would never see the grand old lady ever again. That sort of news comes hard to a youngster.

Well, what to do? I couldn't continue to mope around all the time, so after a few days of mourning I began to put my young life back on track. It was the middle of summer, so school was still a safe month and a half away, so I sought out my friends as a means to heal the wounds.

One evening about a week later we were all playing tag on a vacant lot and I happened to meet a new girl whose family had just moved in. Her name was Carmen and she was about a year older than me. She played tag real well and was faster than most of the kids including me, so I immediately respected her. After the game was over and I started home, she asked me to come over to her house the next day. I said yes without thinking, but the next morning in the sunlight I really felt foolish knocking on a girl's front door!

She invited me in to meet her mother and then we went out into her back yard to play. We played catch and quoits for awhile, but when she asked me if I wanted to shoot her BB gun, things really got interesting! Carmen—a girl—had a BB gun! Yes, she did! She said her father wanted her to learn how to shoot, so he gave her both a BB gun and a .22. She was allowed to shoot the BB gun in the yard, but for the .22 she had to wait until her father could take her someplace to shoot.

We shot all that morning and I was in heaven once again. Carmen taught me some shooting rules her dad had taught her and I followed them to the letter because I didn't want to embarrass myself in front of this girl who I was beginning to fall in love with. She was a much better shot than I, but she showed me how to shoot without lording it over me. The rest of that day was a blur, but I know I spent it with Carmen, along with every day after that.

About a week before school began again, my mother finally met Carmen—something I had been trying to avoid as long as possible. She didn't embarrass me in front of my friend, of course, but when my dad came home that night she lowered the boom. They talked about Carmen after I went to bed, but I was too interested not to sneak out into the hall and listen to what was said. My mother didn't like "that girl," and was afraid she was leading me astray. If she only knew Carmen had a BB gun! I managed to keep that part a secret, but it didn't change anything. In the end, mother had her way and I had to stop going over to Carmen's house altogether.

When school began again, I saw Carmen at lunch the first day. We talked for a bit, but I was too embarrassed to tell her what had happened, so I suppose I sounded foolish. Within a few days, she was hanging around with a different crowd of older kids, and all we saw of each other was when we passed in the hall.

I was in eighth grade that year and Carmen was a freshman in high school. All six grades were combined in one large building at our school, so I still saw her, but as the year progressed, the demarcation between high school and junior high rose up like a stone wall. It programmed all of us so indelibly that we carried it into our adult lives.

I was so brokenhearted throughout the final years of my primary school that I never again socialized with the other kids. When my family finally moved to another state, I used the move to reinvent myself and leave my old personality behind.

I finished school in Oregon, thousands of miles from my Indiana beginnings, and millions of miles from my childhood. Never again was I able to shoot with the freedom I had known back then for such a short time, so when I moved out of the house, I immediately began buying firearms of all kinds. I immersed myself in shooting for about ten years, trying to make up for what I felt I had missed as a child. But it was all to no avail. Firearms are so different from the gentle airguns that they really don't serve as substitutes. I suppose they did get under my mother's skin, which was a pretty good side benefit, but the satisfaction I was seeking was not there. So eventually, I abandoned the shooting sports altogether and took up other hobbies.

Then one day in 1972, a neighbor of mine showed me a pellet rifle he had recently bought from some place back east. It was as heavy as a firearm but as silent as I remember my Daisy being. And the darned thing shot accurately, too. I asked him where he bought it and before the next month was out, I had one just like it.

Since then, I have rediscovered the world of airguns. I now have several old Daisys and other makes of BB guns. They don't shoot quite as well as I remembered, but then, neither do I anymore. I keep them for sentimental reasons.

But I have many accurate and powerful pellet rifles. Most are from Germany, but a few were made in England, and I even have a couple from the good old US of A. These I shoot constantly. They don't replace my lost childhood, but they do make my waning years more enjoyable.

My mother passed away in 1968. We never reconciled our differences, but I do understand her better now that I'm older. She was a product of her upbringing, and in many ways she was very afraid of the world she lived in. Her eccentricities were a defense against many fears.

I never found out what became of Carmen, but I like to think she is married with children (and now grandchildren) of her own and that she is the kind of mother I wish I had. I never married, so this branch of our family ends with me. If Carmen can build a better life for her family than the one I had, then maybe there is hope for the world.

Aurora, Colorado, 1998

Chapter 11
Straight shooter

When I was a boy, I wanted a BB gun in the worst way. Most of my friends had them and it was hard to go out in the neighborhood, unarmed as I was. Most kids figured my folks were poor, which we weren't. Mom just didn't see why her house should be an armed camp, and I think my old man went along with her to keep the peace. She had a formal living room that we kids weren't allowed to play in, and it was loaded with bric-a-brac and other breakable things. I got the impression that she thought I would start sniping at her stuff if I was armed.

My dad would take me down to the local quarry on weekends, where we would both shoot his .22 Winchester automatic. It was lots of fun, but the shells cost a bundle, so I think he resented having to pay so much all the time. One day, while we were out shooting he said, "Bobby, I think it's time we got you a BB gun. Don't you?"

Well, there was no thought required for that! I was for the idea even before he brought it up.

"But what about Mom? You know how she feels."

"Yes I do. Your mother was raised in a different kind of family than ours, son. Her father was a minister, and her mother was a very formal lady. You've seen them when we visit, and they've become more open and friendly over the years."

I thought about that. My grandfather Amos was the sternest man I had ever known. I couldn't ever remember him smiling, and he sure wasn't the guy to be flip with. I even thought my dad was afraid of him.

"In their home, children were either doing their chores, studying their homework or else reading the Bible. There was no time for the things you and your friends like to do."

"Geez, dad, I sure wouldn't have wanted to live like that."

"Your mother is still learning how to relax and have a good time, Bobby. She has a lot of fun in her soul, but her upbringing goes against it, so she doesn't always show her brighter side. I'll tell you what we need to do, you and I. We need to come up with a good reason for you to have a BB gun, one that your mother can agree with. If she could see the practical benefit to your having a gun, I don't think there would be a problem. Can you help me with that?"

I said I could, although I had absolutely no idea how to convince her. It wasn't that she disliked guns the way some mothers did, because she didn't. She just saw no redeeming value to a child's toy like a BB gun, and what couldn't be justified as having practical value in her mind wasn't right. That was a harder nut to crack than just not liking guns, because you didn't know where to begin.

I thought about the problem all the next week. I observed Mom more closely than ever, trying to figure what made her tick. I knew we had to do it right the first time or we would ruin the chance of me ever getting a gun, because once she made up her mind about something there was no changing it.

There had to be some work that only a BB gun could do that Mom would find invaluable. If there was something like that, she might be convinced to relent and let me have one. But what can a BB gun do that can't be done with a hundred other things? I thought about mice and how she hated them. They were forever getting into our dried food in the cellar and ruining things. Mom wasn't afraid of them the way they picture women in cartoons. She didn't jump on chairs or anything; she just hated the damage they did to our food. If she saw one in the cellar, she would get a broom and chase it until it either got away or she killed it. Then she got a cat to patrol the house, but he wasn't much of a mouser. I figured he was afraid of them, because he was always somewhere else whenever there was a problem.

Occasionally, we would get a black snake in the cellar, but that happened too infrequently to be of much help. Dad would have to catch it and take it outside, and I was eventually promoted to the job, after I started school. A snake could ruin an entire Saturday, because the darned things could slither out of sight at a moment's notice. I always got them in the end, but they just weren't the kind of nuisance I needed to justify my getting a gun.

The only other thing that was a possibility was rats. We kept chickens for the eggs and for an occasional roaster, and chickens bring on rats faster than anything I know of. Our coop was always in danger from them. They could kill a young hen in a minute, and the chicks had no chance at all.

Our cat was of no help against the rats, because he was more afraid of them than they were of him. I once saw one of them back him right up when he inadvertently cornered the animal outside the coop. He hissed and snarled, but the rat stood its ground and even advanced, until Mr. Kitty turned and ran away. If I could kill rats with a BB gun, Mom would have to agree.

I told Dad my idea the next time we were out shooting and he thought it was a great one. "We'll have to convince her that you're a good enough shot to do the job, though. She wouldn't say yes unless she thought you could kill them humanely. Let's see how good you are."

He put up a small tomato paste can on the hill we shot into, then we walked back about 100 feet away. I had never tried something that far away before. With his Winchester, you could just keep pulling the trigger until you eventually hit what you were shooting at. First shot hits were never my strong suit, and I suppose that is why my dad suggested it in the first place.

I worked harder that afternoon than I ever had before. I wasn't just shooting. I was shooting to earn my new BB gun. I had to hit the can to win it, and I had to learn to shoot in order to hit. If I had ever spent as much time learning arithmetic as I did learning to shoot that afternoon, I guess I would have made my living doing sums.

Finally, at the end of the day, I got to where I could hit the can three times out of five. I was pretty satisfied with myself, but dad wasn't through with me yet.

"Next Saturday, we'll try it from farther away. You're coming along well, Bobby. You should be able to hit your mark in a few more weeks."

A few more weeks! I had just made a series of near-impossible shots and now he wanted me to do even better! Who did he think I was— Annie Oakley?

I managed to conceal my disappointment only because the cause I was fighting for was such a worthy one. My friends took pity on me for some reason the next week and let me shoot their guns more than ever before. Because I had trained so hard at the gravel pit, I figured I could shoot their BB guns better than they could, but they all outshot me easily.

It turned out that each boy had learned how his gun worked so well that he knew where the BB was going even before he pulled the trigger. Jimmy Rutherford had a Daisy repeater that shot to the left. He had bent the front sight to correct it, but that gun still shot to the left. The farther away you shot, the more left it went, but Jimmy knew exactly where to aim to hit his target. He could hit the tips of kitchen matches at 15 feet, or dimes at 30 feet. I couldn't see how he did it, except that he really knew his gun.

Dale Swartz had an old King single shot that his dad had owned as a kid. It was all beat-up looking, but Dale could hit even better than Jimmy. He said the secret was in shooting lead shot instead of steel. He said steel went faster, but lead went straighter, and his old gun sure proved it! I saw him shoot a bottle cap off a log at 50 feet. Even Jimmy couldn't do that all the time, but Dale sure could.

Steve Sgouri had the most powerful gun of all, although it wasn't the most accurate. His dad bought him a Benjamin pneumatic gun for his ninth birthday. He pumped it on the ground with a long plunger in the nose of the gun, then dropped a lead BB down the barrel. His gun would go through one side of a tin can at close range—something the other boys' guns couldn't do. But Steve was lucky to hit a quarter-sized washer at 20 feet because that Benjamin had a trigger that had to be yanked instead of pulled easily. If you tried for a smooth shot it hissed and the air ran out without shooting the BB.

I tried all their guns, but the experience left me wondering what kind of gun I should get. None of them were as easy to shoot as my dad's .22, and I wasn't even good enough with that yet. So, would I ever be good enough to get a BB gun? I was starting to think I wouldn't.

We went out shooting the next Saturday, and I surprised both my dad and myself with how much better I had become. All that practice with those quirky BB guns of my buddies had made me appreciate what a real accurate gun could do. I began hitting the tomato paste can at 150 feet with regularity, and even as often as my father. So he said it was time to bring up the matter to my mom.

That evening, he got her started talking about the rats, and she went on for quite a while by herself. Four of her chicks were missing and she knew the rats were getting them. She sometimes heard the hens squawking and making a fuss, but whenever she got out to the coop, there was nothing to see. She did see the rats hanging around the compost pit where she threw her edible garbage, though, and since the pit was close to the coop, she was sure the rats were up to no good.

When dad brought up the subject of killing them with a gun, though, she said absolutely not. We lived in town and she didn't want to scare our neighbors with the noise. Besides, she said, a gun wasn't safe that close to town.

Dad agreed with her that a .22 wasn't the thing to use. But he suggested that if they got me a BB gun and I were appointed as the official rat killer, the problem might just be over. Mom said she didn't think a BB gun could kill a big rat, but dad told her it could. She said if it could kill them cleanly she wouldn't mind me having one, but she would have to be convinced that it could. Apparently, that was the moment dad had been waiting for.

Mom allowed as how it probably was even harder to kill a rabbit than a rat—even a big one.

Dad got up from the table and went up to the attic, where we heard him bumping around for a few minutes. Neither my mother nor I knew what he was up to. When he returned, he had a box of old pictures. In it he found an old-time picture of a boy holding a BB gun and standing next to a large dead rabbit.

"That's a picture of me when I was eight years old. My mother bought me a Sentinel BB gun to help keep rabbits out of her vegetable garden one summer. She thought I would just sting them with it, but I soon learned my gun well enough to kill them dead with one shot to the head. She was so proud of me that she had this picture taken with my first kill. If it hadn't been in the summertime, I think we would have eaten that rabbit and all the others I shot, as well.

I was stunned! My dad had been the same kind of boy all my friends were and I never knew it. He had a gun that he learned as well as they all knew theirs and he used to take big rabbits with it. I knew he was a good shot from our time at the quarry, but I had no clue he was that good.

My mom must have been impressed, too, because she said yes to my getting a gun right away. In fact, she went along with me and dad when we went into town to buy it. We looked at lots of BB guns in several different stores and the one we settled on was a Daisy model 25 pump. According to the man at the store, Daisy had just made it easier to cock, and it already had a reputation as one of the hardest-shooting BB guns ever made.

I told him I wanted to shoot lead shot in it, and he turned to my dad and said, "Your boy here knows a lot about BB guns. This gun is made to shoot lead shot only, which is why it is so accurate and powerful. I think this is the gun you want."

The gun was so beautiful I couldn't believe I was getting it. It was long and sleek and looked almost exactly like a pump shotgun my dad owned. Instead of being nickel-plated like most BB guns in those days, it was beautifully blued. It fit me perfectly, although I will admit that the cocking really put a strain on my arm.

Back at home, I shot that gun during all my free time, until I knew where it was shooting without thinking about it. I used the sights, but they seemed to line up for me without much trying. My friends were all envious of my new gun, and I let them all shoot it, too, as they had actually helped me get it. In time, my arm must have gotten stronger because I can't remember that the cocking was that much of a chore for very long.

Within a week of bringing it home, I killed my first rat behind the chicken coop. It was almost too easy, because they weren't afraid of me or anything. My mom taught me how to pick them up with a stick and put them into a burlap feed sack, which had to be buried so the others couldn't get at it. Rats eat their dead, and I sure didn't want to be feeding the colony.

In all, I killed more than 50 of the disgusting things before they seemed to be gone. From time to time after that, if we saw signs of a new one, Mom would immediately deputize me until it was gone.

I was so happy to have my mom's blessings for that gun that the idea of causing trouble with it never entered my mind. Other boys often got in trouble with their guns, but I treated mine as a special tool I was privileged to own and use. I kept it oiled and clean and never once did it stay outside overnight, the way some guns did. As a result, I still have that BB gun today.

I once asked my mom about that time after I grew up and she said something that surprised me. She said, "Your dad and I always wanted to give you a BB gun, but you didn't seem responsible enough for one. Your dad took you down to the quarry to teach you how to shoot, but he said you were too interested in spraying bullets all over the place to hit anything. Then, he got the idea that if you had to work for your gun, you might pay attention to what he was trying to teach you, so he used that little fib about me to get you to think about what you were doing. It worked, too."

El Paso, Texas, 1957

Chapter 12

Values

I looked like a Russian commissar in that picture, with my peasant cap, long field jacket and canvas leggings. Actually, my aunt made that outfit for me, and she decorated it with insignia from old army field units. But she never quite got the look of the coat right, in my mind. I was supposed to be a cavalryman on a western outpost, but I guess she took that to mean the steppes of Siberia.

Everybody asks me who the dog is, but I can't remember. He just came up as the picture was taken. I don't remember him at all, but I suppose he lived close by.

I shouldn't complain about Aunt Olive, either, because in many ways she was like a mother to me. My real mother died shortly after I was born, so I was sent to live with my aunt and uncle until my father could take care of me. Apparently that never happened because I only saw him at holidays, and just for a little while then.

But life was good, nevertheless. My Uncle Dick owned a farm in upstate New York, and I grew up among the salt of the earth. By the time I was ten, I could handle a team, bale hay all day and work alongside any full-grown man. Not that I had to, mind you. My aunt and uncle took good care of me, as though I was their own. They had a son who died in the Great War, and I think I sort of took his place when I came to live with them.

Aunt Olive was a strict disciplinarian who was feared by most of the kids in our neighborhood, but she was always soft on me for some reason. In fact, she made that tent I was playing in, and she used real heavy canvas material in it. It was waterproof in all but a downpour, and many a night I slept outside in it with just my dog, Harvey, to keep me company.

The BB gun was a hand-me-down from someone in the community. I never learned exactly who. There wasn't a lot of money in those days, and new Daisy or King BB guns cost several dollars apiece, which was money we didn't have. But someone had that old Columbian model M laying around and I guess they figured a young boy could put it to some good use. And that was the truth!

Although it was partly broken and would no longer feed BBs, it worked perfectly well when a single BB was dropped down the barrel. It shot hard and straight, and the nickel plate that was still on it was as bright as the day it was made. It out-shot the few Daisys in our neighborhood, except for a new pump gun that was its equal. The kid that owned that gun was from a rich family who gave him whatever he wanted, so there was no way of my keeping up with him. Except for one thing. He liked my gun—a lot. He thought it looked like a real western gun while his looked like a Winchester .22 from a shooting gallery. I tormented him about that whenever possible, of course.

The torment extended to bicycles as well. I had none, while he had the latest model with balloon tires and an electric light. He rode it every day in the summer, while most of the rest of us made do on shank's mare. It always took us longer to go anywhere, so we made him the scout for the neighborhood. If we wanted to go swimming, we sent him on ahead to be sure the pond was open before hiking the mile to it. If there was a circus in town, he rode to where they were set up and reported back to us what attractions they had, when they would open and so on. He never tired of his assignments and it took a lot of pressure off the rest of us.

Except for one thing. He liked to play cowboys and he wanted to carry my gun while he rode. I loaned it to him once, but I was afraid that he would scratch it when he stopped his bike. Instead of coming to a straight stop, he used to jump off to the left side of the bike and stand on the pedal while leaning the bike way over to the right. It made the gravel fly and looked like a horseman dismounting while still at a full gallop, but sometimes he misjudged the ground and lost his balance doing it. He always had skinned up knees and elbows, and I was afraid he would scratch up my rifle, too.

Well, denying him what he wanted was the worst thing I could have done. It made him want my gun even more. He offered to trade me his gun for it, even though he knew my gun didn't repeat and his did. That was how crazy he was. I refused because I didn't really feel as though the gun was mine to deal with. The way it was given to me, I felt it could be taken back at any time, that I was just a temporary custodian.

But he still persisted. He raised the offer to include a nice pocketknife and a big glass cat's eye boulder marble I liked. I continued to say no.

Then one day, my Aunt Olive called me inside for a talk. She asked me what I was doing to Todd—that was the boy's name—to get him so riled up. Apparently, he had gone to his parents over the matter, and they brought it to the attention of my aunt! This was a serious breech of childhood etiquette. We all knew that whatever differences we might have, we kept them to ourselves. Adults were never called into the picture unless the customary warning, "Aww—I'm tellin'!" was issued first. That allowed the other kid time to get his story straight before things got serious.

Trapped as I was by this unexpected turn of events, I became completely flustered and blurted out the truth. I told her about him wanting my BB gun and all the stuff he had offered for it. She asked if he was offering me a good deal. I said yes, but then I told her how I felt about my gun, that it wasn't really mine to trade. She laughed at that and said there had been some sort of misunderstanding. The gun was mine and I could do whatever I liked with it. If I wanted to trade it to Todd, I could.

I went back outside and thought about it for a while. If I traded with Todd, I would have the nicest new BB gun in the neighborhood, instead of one that had to be babied and coaxed. I would also have a truckload of other neat stuff, because he had continued to raise the offer. I reckoned I might even talk him out of a bicycle, along with his Daisy. Not his good bike, to be sure, but Todd had other bikes his folks had given him over the years, and any one of them was better than my current nothing. It was very tempting.

But then I figured Todd could have almost anything he wanted by just asking for it. The only reason he couldn't have a gun like mine was they didn't make them any more. Mine was the only one around, and that made it unique. And, if we did trade, his folks could just buy him another Daisy pump, so I wouldn't have anything special after that.

My aunt had said the rifle was mine to do with as I pleased, so what I was pleased to do in the end was to keep it. There was nothing Todd could do about it. Not with all his folks' money could he own the thing he coveted the most—a thing I had regarded as a hand-me-down until that time.

As you might expect, he fussed and fumed about the situation. Some of the other kids thought I was crazy for not giving in, but it made me very satisfied to know I had something Todd could never have.

My aunt and uncle never said another word to me about the incident, but soon after it happened I found myself being showered by little gifts like the uniform in the picture. I think Aunt Olive was secretly glad I hadn't given in, for some reason.

I got a bicycle not long after that. It was a used one, of course, but it worked well enough to propel me into the ranks of Those Who Rode, which was the difference between the haves and the have-nots in our neighborhood. I often rode it with my Columbian BB gun strapped across my back, just like a real cowboy.

Todd did ruin his BB gun, just as I predicted. But it didn't seem to bother him. He got something else to replace it. And when we were older, his folks bought him a Harley Davidson motorcycle. He was the first kid in our county to have a vehicle of his own. My aunt and uncle didn't even have a car until years later.

I lost track of him after we both turned twenty and began our grownup lives. I still thought about him, though, and knew wherever he was going, he was always going there first class.

Many, many years later, after I grew into manhood, I still had that old Columbian BB gun from my childhood. By then it was worth several times what a Daisy pump was. Daisys were common and the old Columbian was special. That's exactly how I always felt about it, too. I may never have had a first class ticket to anywhere, but I know the value of things, which I think is the better gift.

Yakima, Washington, 1960

Chapter 13
Young hunter

In the picture you will see the two things that were my most prized possessions as a boy—my BB gun, which I always had with me and my dog, Jipper, who was really more of a friend than a possession, now that I think about it. Jipper and I would play hard all day long, going far out into the fields near my house to explore and discover whatever we could find.

I can't say as I remember the shirt or short pants I was wearing that day, but the hat was mine and seldom off my head. People wore hats in those days. In fact, if you went outside without one, you were looked at as strange. Mine was a broad-brimmed felt job that kept the sun out of my eyes, because we didn't have sunglasses out in the country. The city people were still wearing the dark blue glasses that had been popular a decade before, but no self-respecting man of the Nineties would be caught dead in a pair. They called you a dude if you wore something strange like that, and dude was nothing to be called, I can assure you.

I can remember being one of the few boys in town who had a BB gun at that time. Some had their father's hand-me-down .22 single shot rifle, but they weren't allowed to shoot it in town like I was. And that is what made owning a BB gun so fine.

On summer mornings when the squawking blue jays would get in the tree outside my bedroom and raise a ruckus, I could take my revenge out the window, if I removed the screen first. I had taken to unlatching it the evening before and just wedging it in place so the next morning I could silently remove it to take a shot at those noisy birds. I think I must have gotten three or four before my mother found out what was going on and stopped me. She didn't like them any more than I did, but she was disconcerted to find dead birds on the ground outside the back door to her kitchen. So, I had to invent another way to ambush them.

I soon learned they loved meat. In fact, any small dead animals like moles, gophers, mice or rats would bring on the jays like a magnet. So I expanded my hunting skills to include those, as well. I could find all the mice and moles I wanted in the kitchen garden which was conveniently located next to the back of our house. I could see them moving the plants around, but if I moved to see where they were they would always be gone by the time I got into position.

Then I got the idea of sitting on top of the back porch roof, where there was a good view of the whole garden. I was looking down into the rows of plants and the small critters were now quite visible to me. I shot loads of them after discovering that, and once my mother learned what I was doing, she not only gave me her blessing, she encouraged me! In fact, she would often bring me a glass of lemonade or a sandwich while I sat out there and watched.

Once I shot a chipmunk outside our coal cellar and started an argument between my parents. My father thought it was a good idea because he said they were digging holes around the foundation of the house, which they were. But my mother said they were so cute they shouldn't be killed. They didn't argue in front of me, of course, but I could hear them when I went to bed, because my room was right above the kitchen where they talked. The outcome of that argument was what triggered my most famous stunt as a BB gunner.

My mother was against my shooting anything that she didn't consider a pest. I told her I figured that gave me an open license to blast my older sister, but she wasn't amused. She said that in the future I would have to clear all game with her.

For several days, I didn't hunt anything at all. The mice and moles were almost gone from the kitchen garden and there was nothing else I was allowed to hunt, so for what seemed like several weeks but was probably only a few days, I was reduced to shooting at clothespins and marbles. After a stint as a hunter of live game, these were poor substitutes. Then one day, everything changed.

My dog, Jipper, was stung by hornets while he was romping in the back yard. He came tearing around to the front of the house and finding no way inside, went off down the street at a fantastic clip. My mother and I both heard him, but he was moving so fast and howling so loud we were temporarily confused as to what to do. Then my mother heard the noise through the kitchen window. It was a loud humming coming from above the window, so she called me and we went up to my room together. There we saw it—a colony of hornets was building a nest on the tall pole that suspended our telephone wires outside the house.

Although our house was not yet electrified, my dad was one of the first people in town to have a telephone installed. It was on the wall in our parlor, and the wires came in from the street through the back yard. There were only 23 other families in town who had phones at that time, but businesses had them and dad wanted to stay in touch. The telephone exchange was only a block from our house, so the connection wasn't hard to make.

The hornets had chosen to build their paper nest on the iron bar that extended off the pole carrying the phone wires, which meant that they now dominated our back door and the yard all around it. We couldn't use the door; we couldn't go into the garden; we couldn't even mow the back lawn close to the house for fear of being attacked.

Now some people who don't know better will tell you that a hornet is the same thing as a yellowjacket, and what's the big deal about them? You get stung by yellowjackets every summer and, although it is painful for a few minutes and itchy for a few days after, unless there are a lot of stings, it's not so bad. Well, hornets are nothing like that.

Yellowjackets are among the smallest of wasps. Most are no larger than a honeybee and many are much smaller. Although they are dangerous in large numbers, they will usually let you alone if you run away from them. Hornets won't. Hornets can grow to a length of more than two inches, which makes them among the largest of wasps, and they are aggressive to the point of being vengeful. They will get after a person or animal like Jipper and chase them for long distances, stinging all the way. They fly fast and they tend to do everything in bunches, rather than individuals. And their sting is one of the most painful you will ever get. All in all, they are very much insects to be avoided.

Father talked to some men at the hardware store about our problem and they told him to forget about it. Just leave the hornets alone and they would eventually die off when the cold weather came. That meant we couldn't go in our back yard near the house all that time. No more gardening, no more using the back door, which we all did. No nothing that had to do with the back of the house.

Father was unwilling to settle for that, but he wondered what else he could do. Nobody in town wanted to mess with a hornets' nest. One man suggested blasting it with a shotgun, but father thought that was too extreme for a house so close to the center of town. He might have been able to get the sheriff to let him do it, because everyone soon knew about our problem, but I don't think he wanted to raise such a ruckus so close too all our neighbors.

He tried feeding them poisoned meat, but the hornets wouldn't touch it. He was going to try a water hose until my mother talked him out of it. She reminded him of the saying, "Madder than a wet hornet". So there we sat, prisoners in our own home, able to come and go by the formal front entrance only and having to have our wits about us when we did even that! Our horses were spooked by the pests when father brought them out to harness them to the carriage, and life was generally miserable that summer.

Then I got an idea. From my bedroom window, I had a perfect shot at the nest which was only fifteen feet away. In the morning, when the night air was still cold, the hornets were slow and sluggish enough to shoot. The problem was, I had to remove the window screen to shoot them, and if they saw me, they would be on me pretty quick. The element of danger was very real and also very exciting.

The first morning I got managed by holding the screen in by tying a string to it and holding the string against the wall with my shoulder while I cocked and shot the gun through an opening I'd made. With a mouthful of shot, I could spit a BB down the barrel and get off a quick shot. They were clustered around the bottom of the nest, but I couldn't see the opening from my window. So I waited until a hornet came walking around the bottom of the nest before I shot him.

They would open their wings for a few seconds before flying off, and that was when I had to do it. One by one I picked them off as they came around the bottom of the nest to get the sun on their wings. But I didn't hit them all. Some were missed, then flew off to God knows where. I think they sounded the alarm to the rest of the nest because they started coming around the bottom in numbers too great for me to keep up, and I had the get the screen back into place real quick. I must say it took real courage to fasten those latches while a dozen angry hornets buzzed around the screen, looking for an opening. Fortunately, the screen fit the window tightly and there were no tears in the mesh.

Within less than a minute after the first hit, there were about twenty angry hornets walking all over the screen, looking for ways to get in. Many others were hovering just outside, waiting for an opening and making a terrible racket. Although I was scared, I had at least learned how to attract them! Then my mother came in my room and screamed when she saw what was going on. I about jumped out of my skin, but the screen still held them off, so nothing else happened. Except she got an idea.

She figured that if I could attract them to my screen so easily, she could blast them with something that might kill them. She made me close my window that day while she thought about what to do. That evening, she and my father went over some ideas and finally came up with what they thought was a good one. They filled an old squirt gun they had with kerosene. Now many people alive today don't believe we had squirt guns before the turn of the century, but we did. They were cast iron gun frames with a rubber bulb in the grip. They worked quite well, although I must say that when Daisy came out with real metal squirt guns a few decades later, they were much better.

The next morning, mother and I worked the screen in my room the way I had the day before. This time, though, the hornets were ready for us. Before I got off a second shot, they were on their way toward the window with murder in their hearts. Mother let them get on the screen, then squirted each one individually with kerosene. They were mad as hell, so they kept coming over until she had squirted several hundred at least. Some fell to the ground under the window, but we couldn't do anything about it as the rest of them were flying all around the yard and the outside of the house.

We spent the rest of that day inside the house, never trusting that it was safe to go out. We kept most of the windows closed, too. At three o'clock, mother phoned my father at his work and told him how it had gone. He decided to stay away until after sundown.

When he came home, he went up to my room to check on the nest and found it abandoned. The next morning before dawn, he and I went outside to see what had happened. The nest was indeed abandoned, but there were hornets walking all over the ground around our back door. They weren't dead, but they weren't flying, either. I was given the job of getting rid of them.

All that day, I sat on the roof of the porch and picked off walking hornets. I went through a lot of shot, and I must have killed several hundred by late afternoon. Then my mother went outside with her boots on and stomped all the rest of them. We picked up as many as we could find and filled a mason jar and part of a second one. Finally we had our back door again and life returned to normal.

That was when my mother took me downtown to have that picture made. She said I was her brave hunter and she wanted to remember that time forever. What neither of us counted on was that one of the dead hornets would end up in the picture, too. It's on the floor, just behind my left shoe, where it must have fallen off when I sat down.

From that day on, my mother never gave me any trouble hunting with my gun. She laid down the rules, and chipmunks were still off limits, but I was free to shoot any and all pests around our house.

About a week after the incident, one of our neighbors, the mother of one of my best friends, called on my mother to tell her they had a hornet's nest outside their house. She wondered whether I could come over and help them get rid of it. My mother told her to just buy her own boy a BB gun and things would take care of themselves. She said that every home needs a hunter, and the other woman should start training hers. I think that was the proudest moment of my young life, because my mother wasn't willing to hire out her young hunter—she needed me too much at home.

Chapter 14
Howard

It was the late fall when that picture was taken. I know because it was November 29th, the day of my seventh birthday. We got up early that day, and I had to put on my very best travel suit so I could have my picture taken downtown. Mother insisted that we all had our pictures taken on our birthday so she could keep track of how we all had grown. With seven children, I suppose it was necessary. Looking back, I'm surprised she could remember our names, let alone our birthdays. But at seven, you take such things for granted.

My governess, Blanche, got me ready for the long ride into the city. I remember the day as a crisp fall day with lots of sun and vivid blue sky, but a cold wind coming off the lake. Of course, in Chicago there was always a cold wind coming from some place.

At breakfast, Mother hinted that there would be a surprise for me downtown, which I took to mean I was finally getting a BB gun. Both my older brothers had them, and I eagerly awaited the day when I would get one of my own. William had a Daisy with an elegant wire stock, and George had a Quackenbush Lightning that worked with elastic bands. William's gun shot harder, but George's was prettier to look at. It was nickel-plated all over and looked very similar to the .22 bicycle rifles that were all the rage. Of course, it didn't knock down they way they did, but he had a small leather case for it, and it was easy to pretend that it was a real rifle.

I wondered what my gun would be. I knew mother and father would buy quality, whatever they got, for if there was ever a thing they drummed into us during those years it was, "Buy quality. It doesn't cost a cent more." The Quackenbush and the Daisy were both quality items, but there were many BB guns that were not as well made. We had a catalog of outing and sports equipment that showed a good many inferior guns that looked as though they wouldn't hold up to any amount of serious use. One of them was even made of wood, if you can imagine that. It looked more like a toy than a real BB gun, but the advertisement proclaimed how powerful and accurate it was. How I hoped my parents would not be taken in by such obvious false claims! As youth will do, I memorized the name of that inferior product—Markham! I vowed to stay away from their BB guns with a passion. Unfortunately, I forgot that the choice was not mine to make.

The team was spirited from the cold that morning, making the ride into town a swift one. I always enjoyed that trip, whether by carriage or by sleigh. Our team was the most beautiful matched chestnuts I ever saw. Not only did they look alike, they were a real team with perfect cadence. Their pace was fast enough to keep from getting boring, but so smooth you could be lulled to sleep if that was what you wanted. Of course, I wasn't about to miss one moment of this special day. Sleep was the farthest thing from my mind.

The houses flashed by and soon they crowded together into tighter clumps, finally surrendering to urban three and four-story red brick buildings. At last, the larger structures of downtown Chicago loomed into view, and traffic squeezed into the noisy jumble of downtown commerce. You don't get the same feeling when riding in a motorcar because the noises are shut out by glass and steel.

We stopped at Father's bank to pick him up for the outing. He always took the day off for our birthdays, which meant an extra bunch of little holidays for him, of course. I think it was one good reason our family was so large.

The next stop was the big one. Marshall Field's on State Street. They were the biggest in Chicago at that time, and my parents always shopped there for major purchases. Mother especially enjoyed going through the Tiffany boutique, which was where our grand electric parlor table lamp with the dragonfly glass shade came from.

But this was my day, and we didn't dally with furnishings. It was straight to the sporting department to select my present. When we arrived in the wooden-paneled room, I looked all over for the Daisy brand I'd come to know and trust from the catalogues—but it was nowhere to be seen. In fact, the dreaded Markham name was so prominently displayed in the BB gun section, they must have been the only brand in the store that day.

I only learned many decades later of the bitter wars fought by various manufacturers that guaranteed exclusivity of certain manufacturers' goods for a period of time in a store—no matter how large the name on the sidewalk outside. These were called department stores, but they did not begin to resemble the department stores we know today. They carried the brands that offered them the most favorable terms at wholesale, and companies would almost kill to get an account in one. So, if there were Markhams in Marshall Field's, you could bank on there being nothing but—that was the way it worked!

Except over at Sears & Roebuck. They carried every brand on the market, to their great credit. A fact that, unfortunately, had absolutely no impact on my situation, for my parents steadfastly refused to give their business to "that peddler." Hence, our family had to buy the goods that Field's was willing to sell, or shop at the smaller stores, or go without. In my case, it meant going without, for there simply weren't any BB guns at the smaller stores. Like it or not, a Markham it had to be.

Ironically, if the item in question had been a particular meerschaum pipe for father or a certain piece of crystal or furniture that mother wanted, there were ways to go around the tyranny of Field's. Both of my parents were skilled in the fine art of rationalization, if it benefited their cause. But a boy's toy gun hardly qualified for such extreme measures. As Father himself said to me on that very day, "One BB gun is as good as another. They're all made in the same factory, you know."

I must have said something to prompt that statement, but the years have erased whatever it was from my memory. I do remember being mighty disappointed on that day, though, and the object of my disappointment was that new gun.

It wasn't one of the all-wood models, thank God. I don't think I could have contained myself if it had been. Instead, it was a wooden-stocked nickeled gun—called a King. Actually, it was a very attractive little gun that I might have enjoyed very much, had the initial introduction been different. Had the gun come in a brightly wrapped box to be opened in the privacy of my home, I might have been quite taken with the obvious beauty and grace of the King, but that wasn't the way it happened. Instead, I felt as if I had been dragged into the pit of hell itself and forced to accept something. How can you do that when you know it comes from hell?

The rest of that day went downhill for me. I can't remember anything specific, just that the day marked the first real disappointment in my young life. There was a party, of course, and other presents as well, but the BB gun was supposed to have been the big one.

I never played much with the King after that. When William and George took their guns out to shoot at toy soldiers in the side yard, I would tag along and borrow shots from them rather than shoot mine. It got progressively harder for me to even look at it because of all the grief it dredged up. So, finally, I snuck up to our attic and put it up on top of one of the crossbeams in a tight place where no adult would ever go. That act released my spirit to feel normal again, and I quickly forgot all about it.

The years passed and other interests came and went. At Manlius Military Academy, I was on the cadet marksmanship team, and followed the exploits of America's finest shooters all over the globe. At Harvard, I shot on the rifle team, where I managed to post some credible scores.

When I returned to Chicago, I entered the same bank where Father had worked and quickly established myself as a likely comer. Weekends were spent at the local rifle club, where I learned to shoot in the old

German fashion with single shot rifles called Schutzens. One time I will never forget; Harry Pope, the great barrel maker and world champion shot, came to our club and shot a demonstration match of 100 shots offhand. After seeing what that man could do with a rifle, I knew I would never amount to more than a casual shooter; but it was still inspiring to keep trying. If men like Pope, who was an MIT graduate engineer, were interested in marksmanship, I was in good company.

Then came a day that all families must endure. Father died suddenly while working in the garden. He was seventy-one, so it was not that shocking, except that there had been no warnings of ill health.

We had suffered death before; my youngest brother, Howard, had died of scarlet fever several years earlier while I was in France fighting with the AEF. He was only 12 at the time. He was so much younger that I wasn't at home while he was growing up, so we weren't as close as brothers usually are. And Father had always been the center of our family. It seemed as though the family ended when he died.

After Father's funeral was over and affairs had been settled, Mother decided to sell our house and move out west to spend her remaining years in Los Angeles. Her sister owned a hotel in a nearby village called Hollywood. She often wrote of the lovely climate and gentle way of life out there.

Mother asked us children to help her settle the house and get it ready for sale. We helped her box and crate the few things she would be taking with her and we helped the estate broker mark everything else for sale. Father had left more than enough money to take care of her, so the money from the sale of house and belongings she divided among the remaining children.

I was sad to see the house I'd been brought up in sold to another family, but I had a family of my own and our home was now the focal point of my life. Just after the old home was sold but before the new owners took possession, I walked the grounds one final time, trying to remember as much of my wonderful childhood as possible. If you've ever returned to the home of your birth, perhaps you have experienced the feeling I am referring to. There were so many landmarks and memories crowding my brain for recognition. I filed them neatly away, promising to remember them from time to time, but knowing I probably never would.

Many, many years later, I think it was just before Pearl Harbor, I chanced to visit the old neighborhood once more. It was business that brought me back, but I remained for a while afterward to look at the old place one last time. I wasn't even living in Illinois any longer, so this was a unique opportunity.

A different family was living there, and they had a young boy of about 11 years. He was out in the side yard doing something rather intently, so he didn't notice when I walked up and stood to watch. He was playing soldiers! I remembered playing soldiers on the same patch of ground forty-five years earlier.

I had shot at Boers then; this boy was shooting at tin soldiers from the Great War! The game was still the same, though. You were a handsome American captain, whom no amount of enemy fire could destroy. Oh, you took a round in the arm or the side from time to time, but that was just to get you into the hospital where you always met a beautiful nurse and got some kind of medal. Then, after recuperating on your back under the hickory tree for five minutes, you were back in the battle.

The enemy was a bunch of stiff tin soldiers who lined up in front of the hedge and allowed you to snipe at them with your BB gun. They shouted vile commands at each other in unintelligible languages until you silenced them with a crack shot that sent them flying twenty feet. Like you, they could recover and return to battle just as many times as you desired.

Most boys used some sort of Daisy gun for this, but I noticed this young man had something quite different. It looked very old, yet familiar. When he paused long enough to notice me standing there, we started up a conversation about playing soldiers and BB guns and so forth.

He said his name was Howard, and his family had moved into the house the previous year. His mother was initially opposed to him having a BB gun, so she told him he could have one, "When the angels came down and gave it to him." While playing in the attic one day, he noticed something laying on top of the crossbeam in a dark corner of the room. He pulled down a dusty red felt bag that contained the gun he was holding.

When he showed it to his mother, she broke into tears upon finding the name "Howard" carved in the stock at the bottom of the pistol grip. Her son hadn't noticed it until she pointed it out. The letters were neat and small, and they were filled with the dark patina of age. It was clear to her that her son could not have put them there.

She said that was good enough for her. He could keep the gun and shoot it. He told me he thought it was the finest BB gun ever made, and, because it had his name on it, he knew it was made especially for him. Everyone in his neighborhood had a Daisy; he had the only King!

I never mentioned the real history of the gun to the boy, because he obviously appreciated it far more than I ever had. I left him playing there in the yard, because I suddenly had my own rush of boyhood memories to deal with.

The one curious thing about this incident was the name carved on the stock. My name is Theodore, and I never carved it on anything. That gun had somehow acquired a history of its own, and I was simply one small part of it.

Chapter 15
The wind gun of Prostl

A fictional account of the development of an early airgun

At no place in the world were more exciting things to be found than in the workshop of August Bidderman, the clockmaker of Prostl. For thirty-five years he had been the region's master clockmaker, producing some of the most wondrous timepieces ever constructed. The most famous of these, of course, was the great cased hall clock he made for Baron Von Eiger, whose huge wooded estate occupied fully a quarter part of the valley in which the ancient village nestled.

That clock was said to not only tell the hour of the day or night with such remarkable precision that astronomers could perform their calculations by it; it was also a thing of enormous beauty, being cased with the finest carved walnut and heavily figured with brass and silver engravings. It stood as tall as three men standing upon one anothers shoulders, and the figures carved in deep relief up the sides told the fictional tale of one of the region's most celebrated heroes.

On the sides of the massive top, crystal windows allowed a view of the magnificent brass works. The height of the case necessitated that one who wished to view the works be elevated more than two tall men's height from the floor, so the Baron had installed a staircase and small balcony on the end of the room, next to where the clock stood, the better to see the curious insides at eye level. The clock's huge weights were brass-bound dressed stones, and the massive brass pendulum was shaped after the baron's family crest.

In fact, that large clock was so beautiful that the Emperor himself coveted it. He did so to such an extent, in fact, that the baron was forced to offer it as a gift less than a year after first installing it in his own great hall.

When the clock was first installed in his hall, the baron invited the villagers in to his hall, to witness the striking of the chimes. Now, however, the clock was never seen, except by nobility and the few clergy important enough to gain admittance to the private chambers of his majesty. Commoners had to content themselves with the faintest whisper of its melodic bells, which could be heard outside the palace grounds on still evenings.

But clocks and the occasional watch weren't the only things the great August Bidderman made. No, indeed! He also made nautical navigating instruments of such tremendous cunning that official commissions came from as far away as England—all passing through the Emperor, of course. Bidderman's instruments were said to be one of the keys that held the English empire together, through the offices of her great navy. Within a few years, they would be combined with the newly-invented chronometer to solve mankind's greatest mystery at that time—the precise measurement of longitude! But even these famed instruments, as wondrous as they were, did not complete the extent of Bidderman's exceptional skill.

The man also made music boxes! These were the closest he came to true witchcraft, for each box seemed to contain a miniature orchestra, so full and complete were the sweet strains that emanated from within. Every box played a program of eight tunes—some with the accompaniment of mandolins that astounded everyone who heard them. How such wonders could be folded up and stuffed into a small pear-wood box that stood on a table was beyond everyone fortunate enough to behold them, but whenever they were played in public, the results could scarcely be refuted. It seemed as if God, Himself, had charged His angels to inhabit the Bidderman boxes, spreading joy to all who had ears.

At this point his greatness finally reached its summit, or so it seemed to all but a very few people. Those who knew Bidderman well enough and were of a station to address the master by his Christian name knew that he also sometimes handled projects of such mystery and complexity that there was no way to categorize them. Among these select few people, the baron was one of the very few with influence enough to get the master to do his bidding. Actually, both influence and money—for Bidderman was human, after all. He had to eat, like everyone else. So, when his patron approached him with a secret commission to make something the world had never before seen, he, alone, possessed the necessary credentials to motivate old August.

The master trained apprentices from time to time, but when the baron made his approach for this commission, he was alone. Perhaps, with what came to pass, that was a fortunate circumstance.

It was late on a frosty December morning in the year 1724 when the baron's carriage drew up to the front of the workshop, located in the same quaint building where the old man rested his head. The day was sparkling clear and of such sharpness that the master bid the nobleman come quickly inside, forsaking the usual pleasantries they might have exchanged on the threshold. The carriage was dispatched on to the village for supplies, and would call for him upon its return, just before the early twilight. Inside, the master found the best chair for his patron, then fetched them both an earthen mug of warm gluhwein while he listened to what the gentleman had to say.

The baron had in his possession a worn wooden case, similar to one the old man might have made for one of his nautical instruments, but both longer and wider. Instead of disclosing the contents, he began with a short story about his cousin, a nobleman from the Low Countries by the North Sea. It seems this cousin had lent some money to another titled man, who, in return, gave him some property to hold for surety. The other man had unfortunately perished from plague before his debt was fully repaid, so the cousin now owned the several items deposited with him. Included in the manifest was a curiosity that he had brought with him to show to the baron.

At this, the gentleman opened the case to reveal a snaphance, or so it seemed at first glance. But for some strange reason, this snaphance had a butt that removed from the works. And, stranger still, the butt was finished with wrought iron!

"Can you guess its purpose?" he asked the now-curious Bidderman.

For a long time, the old clockmaker spoke not a word. The silence was punctuated only by the rhythmic beat of the shop clock on the wall. He took out his magnifying lens, the better to examine the inner workings of the quaint piece, but to no avail. Although it had the unmistakable lines of a snaphance, there was no place for the flint to be held and no touchhole for the priming charge. This was no snaphance. He looked puzzled.

"I'll give you some help," the baron finally said. From the same wooden box, in a separate compartment, he produced a tubular object to which he affixed two ebony handles.

"I know what that is", Bidderman proclaimed with a sly smile. "It's a condensing syringe. I've seen one at the university. They condense wind into a small vessel, where it can be stored until its release."

"You are correct, my old friend," said the younger man with a smile. "Now, can you tell me why this syringe is needed for this snaphance?"

"My lord, I would never try to fool you. I do not have the vaguest notion of what that syringe has to do with this strange snaphance, if that is what it is."

"It has everything to do with it, Bidderman. For you see, this is not a snaphance at all. It's actually a gun that fires, using just the wind!"

The look the old man gave him was so unmasked that his young patron had to laugh. He didn't believe it! A gun that fired with wind only was beyond the pale of even Bidderman's powerful magic. He simply did not believe such a thing was possible. This the baron had anticipated, for he, himself, had doubted what his cousin told him until the piece was actually demonstrated. So, he proceeded to do the same for the old artisan.

First, he opened a small silver vessel and dropped a few drops of what smelled like sperm whale oil into the iron fitting at the end of the butt. Then, he dropped some more oil into the end of the syringe. After that, he screwed the syringe to the gun's butt until the joint between them was invisible. A flat plate was then screwed onto the other end of the syringe. Now, he placed the flat plate of the syringe on the floor of the workshop, holding the end of the syringe nearest the butt by the two wooden handles and proceeded to pump up and down many, many times. They both lost count, but the total number of pumps certainly numbered in the hundreds.

He then removed the syringe from the butt and replaced it with the lock and barrel of the gun. Then, he loaded a patched lead ball into the muzzle, and, after ramming it home in the usual fashion, asked where he might safely discharge the piece.

Bidderman thought he was being hoaxed, so he casually indicated the front door of his shop, whereupon the baron immediately shouldered the weapon and fired it! To Bidderman's utter astonishment, the gun actually fired, discharging its ball deeply into the thick oaken door panel with an astonishing boom!

After some moments passed and he was fully in control of his senses once more, the old craftsman went over to the door to examine the hole made by the ball. It was so deep that he couldn't even see the tip of the lead. He took a sharp chisel from his bench and carefully cut around the hole until he had the lead ball in his hand. It had penetrated the hard oak door panel to a depth of the first joint of his little finger. Such power had come from nothing more than condensed wind!

"Please shoot it again, my lord," old August exclaimed. The younger man complied, and for the rest of that afternoon the two men occupied themselves with the curious wind gun from the Low Countries.

Finally, the baron revealed his true reason for coming. He said he had attempted to purchase the gun from his cousin, but the man was adamantly opposed to selling it at any price. He did, however, graciously agree to leave it with Von Eiger until the Spring Festival, so he might enjoy the piece for a time.

"What I want is for you to make such a weapon for me. I will pay your costs and a great deal more if you can do it. Do you think you can?"

Bidderman had anticipated this request. Indeed, even if the baron had gathered up the gun and left his workshop right then, the old man would have felt compelled to try to make one. All the better that the piece would be in his care for a time so he could study it at great length. "I will make such a piece or better for you, my lord. And, it will be costly, for I know not the art by which such a thing is made to work.

Much of what I must do is to learn this new business before I can attempt to put it to use in any practical fashion."

"All this I know, old master. I am willing to pay your price, for you have always been just in your accounting with me. The only thing I must insist is that you not reveal what you are doing for me. No one must learn of this commission, or of the existence of the wind gun. You will no doubt recall how easily the Emperor talked me out of the fine cased hall clock you made for me? I had it less than four full seasons before he snatched it away to his private chambers. If he were to learn of this commission or of the existence of this wondrous arm, I would never be permitted to retain it for myself."

"I have often wondered why you did give him the clock, my lord. You paid so much for it and waited seven long years while I worked out the mechanism and carved the case and faceplate. What could possibly have moved you to part with something so dear?"

"What, indeed, Bidderman? How about my estate, and all that goes with it?"

"Are you saying the Emperor would have deprived you of your birthright?"

"Not directly, perhaps, but just as certainly, yes. You see, after viewing that splendid clock in my grand hall, his majesty revealed to me that he was soon to select the land needed by the royal army to use as a training ground for their horses. He confided that the decision came down to three parcels of land, one of which was in the heart of my own estate!"

"But he can't just take your land, can he, my lord?"

"No, he can't just take it. But what he can do is declare the property he needs as essential to the crown and compensate me with a stipend. Typically, I would receive one-fourth what the land would bring if a private individual purchased it. It is my station and duty to put the needs of the crown before my own, no matter what the consequences. The Emperor knows I could not refuse such an official request. Losing that land would bankrupt my family!"

"I think I understand, my lord. The crown would take your land at one-fourth its true worth, and all you would have would be the pittance they chose to pay you."

"If that were all there were to it, I would even have no complaint. No, the damage the loss of land would do to my position is much worse. I make money from my estate—from hunting and fishing leases, farming rights, timber sales, the toll road that runs through it that I maintain and such. If I were deprived of what is essentially the heart of my finest lands, much of what I bring in would be lost forever.

"On the other hand, my estate must pay an annual tax to the crown, in return for protection from invasion, the rights I have at court, and so on. That tax is assessed against my title, without regard to the status of my estate. If I cannot pay the tax, the crown has the right to seize my property, including all my land, my home and all the chattels I possess. I would retain my title, but it wouldn't bring me a single copper penny. I'd be without means of support, like the noblemen you hear about in the great towns who must marry off their daughters to wealthy merchants in order to provide for them. Titled families are destroyed when that occurs. So, you see why I gave up the clock to save my lands, despite the anguish it caused me."

"I had no idea, my lord," the old man said.

"Of course you didn't, my friend. As a freeman and as the master clockmaker in the land, you are insulated from such travesty. The Emperor would never treat you in this manner, for fear you might steal away to England and profit their monarch instead of him. Your wealth is in what you can do, Herr Bidderman. You carry it with you, in your hands and your head. Mine, unfortunately for me, is in my title, which is tied to my estate. One less nobleman is of but little consequence to the crown, for the land remains where it is at all times. So you can see why I don't want word of this work falling into the wrong hands. I could end up paying for the Emperor's next new toy."

The old master looked into the young baron's eyes for a long moment before speaking. "You have my word, my lord. No one will know of this work."

His noble guest departed soon after their conversation, leaving the craftsman to ponder far into the evening on the lesson he had just received. Always, in his dreams, he had imagined himself born into nobility, able to enjoy life without a care. How wonderful it must be to eat choice cuts of meat and be pampered by servants who jump at your slightest beck. Furs for clothing and the finest of wines and spirits. A woman to tend the fires and throw furs on the floor so the nobleman never had to get cold feet. No ice in the wash basin, and a chambermaid to rinse the night soil from the chamber pot! Never in all his dreaming, however, had he imagined it might be worse to be somebody who actually owned something of value, because it attracted thieves in imperial purple.

He spent the rest of that Yuletide season studying the strange wind gun, which revealed its secrets rather sooner than expected. It was really quite a simple mechanism, and, although fashioned with some care, he saw ways in which the basic wind lock might be improved. It was his gift that once a mechanism was revealed, he could see many ways to improve it. Sometimes, those changes might themselves engender other improvements, once the clumsiness of the original design was swept away.

Indeed, some days the old man would sit for hours looking at the rough-hewn wall behind his workbench, his eyes unfocused while his mind saw things he could not put into words. If a person were to see him at these times, they would see his hands tracing a phantom mechanism or working a phantom fixture that was still to be built, and even then he was improving upon that which did not yet exist.

Knowing that his time with the piece was limited, he filled many parchments with notes, until it looked to him as though he might actually build the gun from the notes, themselves. Of course, such a thing was unheard of. To make a thing, you either had to have another one in front of you to copy, or you had to have such a clear idea in your mind that you could make it from memory. A master like August Bidderman could do the latter, but only because he had done the former so many times before.

As winter warmed into early spring, he began to have flashes of an idea for a wind gun that carried the idea beyond the example he still possessed. He began to picture a way to channel the wind so that he could control it far more closely than did the lock on the gun from the Low Countries.

On some days, he would arise with some small part of the idea in his mind. This he committed to parchment, as though the actual gun he was imagining were in his hands. He couldn't see all of it at any one time, but he had faith that his great mind was nevertheless designing the entire piece for him. If he hadn't been a clock maker with masterpieces to his credit he would have shrugged off this strange sense of clairvoyance and stuck to what was before him, but from experience he knew he could trust his instincts.

So, on one fine day very near the time of Spring Festival, he made a call upon his patron in the great hall. That afternoon, in the formal garden, he explained to the young nobleman as best he could that he could make a wind gun that would be superior in all respects to the example left by the cousin.

Von Eiger was greatly disappointed at hearing that the old master had not been busily making his gun all this time. Instead, he learned that not one piece of work had actually been started and all that existed were a pile of parchment drawings and arcane notes.

Still, he was well-acquainted with the reputation of the craftsman, having seen wondrous things come from his rude workshop. Might the old man make a wind gun that was as advanced as the great clock he had lost forever? If Bidderman felt that strongly about it, then there must be something to it. He agreed to let old August deviate from simply copying the existing wind gun and take this new direction. Within days, the idea began to take form.

The original wind gun was returned to his noble cousin who packed it into his baggage when his carriage set off for home at the end of Festival. The master continued his work in secrecy, reporting progress to the baron at discreet encounters.

At one of these meetings, he informed his patron that he had secured a supply of Spanish steel, quite similar to the very substance from which those wizards made their famous blades. He had learned enough of its secrets to risk making the new wind gun from steel rather than iron, which any other craftsman would have used. The cost was stunning, but the baron was thus assured he was getting the best the old man could make.

Several weeks later, however, when the baron happened by the workshop, he took immediate note of the crestfallen look on the master's countenance. It was quite impossible, he was informed, to bend the steel of the lock in the fashion that he would normally use to bend iron. And the bend was essential to his plans!

The reason, he was told without understanding a tenth of it, was that steel depended upon a very specific content of chimney soot for its strength. He didn't see how that was possible, for you certainly couldn't see the soot within the silvery metal, but the master swore it was there. It was one of the secrets of Spanish steel. To heat the metal of the lock sufficiently to bend it to the proper angle would drive out most of the soot from the steel, leaving a poorer iron in its place.

Somehow, the tough steel lock had to be bent without resorting to heat. But that was impossible, Bidderman exclaimed. The reason he had wanted to use steel in the first place was because it didn't bend! Yet his design required that it did. If he bent it in the usual fashion, it turned into the basest metal, hardly fit for door hinges, to say nothing of the masterpiece for which it was intended.

The baron took pity on his old friend and took him to the gasthaus Grosse Bär in the village where they shared a radish on buttered rye with several tankards of beer from his own brewhaus. He let the older man pour out his heart, which, as the strong amber beer took effect, changed from remorse to mild humor.

Finally, the baron spoke but a single thought—one that would have an everlasting impact upon history. He said, "A pity old Archimedes isn't here to hear you shout 'Eureka' on the day you finally solve this problem, my friend." He thought he was only consoling the old man, but fate thought different.

The next day, old August Bidderman went to work in his shop with renewed vigor. He needed a powerful screw, and he needed to attach to it a long lever—the kind with which Archimedes might have moved the world. Together, they might just provide the mighty force required to bend the solid steel lock while it was still as cold as stone. But where to get one?

He knew that printers had large screws to run their presses. But the force he required went so far beyond any printing press he knew of that the comparison was only in kind. He needed a much larger screw than any printing press.

His answer might lie in the university. They had a machine that generated huge forces by means of a mechanical screw. Could he "borrow" just the screw? No, he could not. It was embedded within a complex press that was too valuable to be dismantled, no matter how skilled the craftsman.

Then, could he use the press? Perhaps. First, the regent would have to be informed of the complete nature of the intended experiment, and of course the university would somehow have to be compensated for the use of their valuable machine. Bidderman knew the regent wanted the money for himself, but he thought he could disguise his work sufficiently to get it past him without comment. The baron could take care of the fee. But when the price was named, it proved too large to even consider approaching his patron.

That left him to his own devices. He would have to construct a press to generate huge forces that were beyond imagination. If only steel weren't so very hard! But that was what made it steel, after all. If only it could be hard under some circumstances and soft under others. On this point, he pondered at length, which gave him an idea. If anyone knew all the properties of steel, it had to be the very same Spaniards from whom his supply of the metal had originally come. He had to talk to one of them who knew how to work the metal. But where would he find such a man? In Vienna, of course.

The city of Vienna was famous as one of the continent's busiest crossroads, even in the early 18th century. Bidderman traveled there by coach, paid for by his patron, who knew as well as he the value of the knowledge he sought. If August said there was something he had to learn before proceeding on the gun, nothing could be allowed to hinder him.

Once in the city, he paid an agent to arrange a meeting with the right people who, as it turned out, were in permanent residence. They had been commissioned by the city elders to construct a wondrous new clock, whose train of steel-shod gears would last a millennium or more. Their knowledge of the metal was encyclopedic, as it had to be, for they were many weeks journey from the source of metal and the legendary foundries of Toledo. Still, they managed quite well with what looked to the uninformed to be a well-provisioned blacksmith's shop. That was where the master of Prostl met with them and that was where the new knowledge was imparted.

"You see, Herr Bidderman, steel is a most complex substance." his tutors explained. "It's nothing at all like the iron from which it is made. Even though the two metals resemble one another closely and both are known to attract the needle of a compass, steel is by far the better material. For strength and durability, it has no equal.

"Now, as to bending it—that is where the nature of the metal is to your advantage. If you are a careful worker, and we know beyond the shadow of a doubt that you are, you can bend the steel as easily as you can iron, yet still retain all the properties of the stronger metal."

With that pronouncement, the Spaniard showed August how, by controlling the temperature of the metal through observation of its color when heated, one could bend it as easily as iron, yet still retain all the precious carbon that gave it its character. No matter how large the piece, as long as the heat was even and controlled and did not go too high, the steel would bend.

Bidderman remained in the city a fortnight, learning all that his funds entitled him to; then he secured passage on the first coach going near his village. Within a week of returning, old August had built the special forge he required to control the temperature precisely. Like the object he was crafting, the secret of the forge was also founded on forced wind. Another two weeks were required to fashion the powerful screw he required, together with the mechanism in which it would operate. Built mostly from iron, he used some of his precious steel to strengthen the parts that would take the largest strain.

As it turned out, the screw he needed wasn't nearly as large as he originally imagined it would have to be. The secret of heating the steel allowed the use of much less force. That was a blessing, because even at its reduced size, making the screw proved a daunting task for the clockmaker. Its scale was beyond what he was used to.

After performing several trials to see that his new apparatus worked as intended, he finally heated the steel lock and bent it to precisely the angle he required. Because of the subtle angle put into the lock, the butt of the gun would rest squarely on the shooter's shoulder while the barrel would point naturally in the direction of the target. The bend was so trivial that August could only see it if he concentrated very hard. He had to use a straightedge to demonstrate its deflection for the casual observer, but since the gun was a secret, the only one he showed it to was the baron. Still, it was this bend—the very whisper of a curve—that gave his weapon the grace of the ages, instead of looking like something a tinsmith had put together.

For a barrel, Bidderman selected a slender brass bar, which he had also obtained while in Vienna. This he heated and stretched by working it over an iron mandrel until it stretched three times its original length. The mandrel left a smooth bore that he could simply freshen with a small cutter, but the master was far from finished with his innovations on this gun. Instead of just reaming out a straight smooth hole as any competent gunsmith would have, he made a tiny cutter to insert into the barrel. By following a carefully made gearing mechanism on the outside of the work, the cutter proceeded to cut a shallow spiral down the inside of the brass tube.

The cutting machine was based on one he used for clock gears, so it was little trouble to index the cutter again and again until the inside of the tube contained an even dozen scratches, all parallel to each other and all spiraling down to the muzzle. These scratches, when properly deepened by repeated cutting, were called rifling, the effects of which had been discovered by the Flemish a century before.

The original thought was that the rifling imparted a spin to the ball, which made it impossible for demons to sit astride as they steered it off its course. No one believed such a myth in the 18th century, however. They had deduced that a spinning ball must act like a child's top, and be better balanced through its flight. Whatever the science, the spinning ball was proven many times more likely to strike the target than one that flew free.

Again and again, Bidderman fed his tiny cutter down each scratch. It was at this point that the precise indexing of his machine paid off, for his eyes could discern none of the grooves yet. Pass after pass of the cutter was made, deepening each groove in turn until it was finally possible to see them all. When he noticed this, he pushed a soft lead ball through the barrel and saw it come out the muzzle with the perfect impression of the rifling engraved on its sides. The Baron would have no trouble hitting what he shot at with this gun! The borrowed wind gun from the Low Countries had a smooth barrel, so already he had kept his promise to make this one better.

The butt of the piece was intended to hold the condensed wind, and must therefore allow none of it to escape. He fashioned it from thick sheet iron, which he folded into a long hollow triangular shape that was locked together at the seam on the bottom with a special mechanical lip and shelf. The butt plate was similarly attached, then brazed with hot brass around its seam to prevent leaks. After two dozen iron rivets had been installed to prevent the long seam on the bottom of the butt from weakening under pressure, it was similarly brazed for integrity. It took no small skill to braze that long seam accurately, but such skill was part of what made the old man the master he was. Now fashioned, the butt was ready to contain the real secret of the gun—Bidderman's special wind-lock valve.

In his dreams about the gun, the master had seen that wind, like all natural forces, moves according to rules that never change. Once, when shooting the prototype gun from the Low Countries, he had chanced a second shot and found it to be nearly as strong as the first. That started him thinking that if the wind was allowed to exit the gun through a portal that remained open for only an incredibly short amount of time, there might be enough remaining in the butt for a second shot. Perhaps even more. He began to think of the wind as he did the water that powered the village mill. It was controlled by the height of the millrace gate and therefore was always moving the mill wheel with the same force, regardless of how high the stream was.

From his clockmaking, old August knew that force was the result of both opportunity and desire. The wind in the butt had a great desire to escape, but it didn't have the opportunity until the valve provided it. By allowing only a small opening to pass the escape hole for a brief moment in time, he could control how much wind was expelled with each shot, thereby leaving some for the next shot.

He made many of the valve parts from brass, for he knew that metal best of all. It would work tirelessly for years without lubrication. It could work at great pressure, so it was perfect for a part that would reside in the butt, where the pressure would sometimes be extreme. But best of all, brass would not corrode like iron and even steel. This was important for a part subjected to the heating of the condensing syringe and the cooling caused by the sudden release of wind at firing. Yes, brass was perfect for this job.

To seal the opening at the tip of the valve, he selected material from the fresh horn of a bull. When cut to size and fitted to the steel rod that passed through the brass valve head, a ring made from bull-horn stopped the flow of air almost perfectly. But almost was not good enough for August Bidderman. He desired a vessel which, when filled with condensed wind, would retain all of it for a full day or even longer. So he turned the steel rod tipped with bull-horn against the brass end of the valve, adding common chalk for lubrication, until the valve screeched like a vixen in the spring. This was the sound that announced a perfect mating of horn to metal. When oiled with a small amount of sperm oil, the valve would contain the wind tightly. Bidderman pronounced the work good, but he did one more thing before moving on.

He removed the brass valve from the iron butt and with a long thin stick he smeared grease on the walls inside the butt. Now, when dirt particles made their way into the butt from the condensing syringe, they would stick to the grease instead of getting into the smooth valve parts to disrupt the seal. The gun from the Low Countries had been treated in this way, and he could see the value when he examined it. Before returning that piece, he had cleaned out the old grease and applied fresh in its place. Such a job might be expected to last for up to five years, depending on the goodness of the grease, how many times the butt was filled and how quickly the grease aged. Except for a covering, the butt was now complete.

The cover was fashioned from the skin of a shark! Bidderman cut the leather to fit, then artfully stitched the seam with the finest deer tendon fiber. Then he immersed the leather covering in water for a day. When it was removed it slipped over the hollow butt and, when dried in the sun, it tightened like any leather would, adding strength to the butt. This material, known as shagreen, was not common in Bidderman's day, but it would become the most popular kind of covering for wind gun reservoirs within the next 50 years.

For the lock and all its working parts, only forge-hammered steel would do. Bidderman carefully heated each part of his lock in the forge then skillfully hammered them into the proper shapes. Files did the finish work, of course, but he wanted to get as close as possible with the forged part to retain the integrity of the metal's own living grain.

One part that almost stumped the old master was the powerful spring to drive the hammer. An ordinary snaphance or flintlock hammer simply causes flint to strike steel with force, but Bidderman's lock required the hammer to push the valve lever through a determined arc against the force of wind trying to escape the butt. That was how the marvelous valve he designed worked. It had to be pushed both open and then be allowed to close by the two-way action of the lever, which was made to operate by the unique shape of the hammer.

To do all that work required a spring that had never before been constructed. Oh, far larger and more powerful springs existed for a long time before this. Coaches had them, as did a number of large mechanical devices. Even large clocks had them. But never before had the power required for Bidderman's lock been made into a spring small enough to fit within the lock he designed. He had to experiment until he got what he wanted.

Weeks went by as the old master labored to fashion that which he had never seen. A few times he lost confidence and had to do other work until his mind had cleared once more. One full year and a part of the next had passed since the baron had given his word to proceed and still the promised gun did not exist. And, unless he could fashion a spring to power it, it never would.

He tried new shapes and sizes but nothing was to any practical avail. The closest he got was a huge spring that was too outsized for any gun. By tying his gun to the workbench and leaving the lockplate off, he could mount this giant spring to the working parts of the lock and get off a shot of wind from the butt before the spring jumped out of position.

What he needed was a spring with the strength of this huge one, yet its size had to be more like that of a firelock spring. He made one that was so thick it stuck out to the side of the lock, but it did remain on when he shot the gun and the whole thing did work. But this fat spring was too ungainly for him to put on anything that bore his own precious name, so back he went to figure something new.

All this power was causing the outside of his comely lock to triple in size. No longer was its elegance visible behind the huge outer housing needed to contain both the huge hammer spring and the trigger spring.

He needed the mass of a large spring to fit into the space of a small one. One day, for no reason he could discern, he remembered his youth as an apprentice sawyer, before he had impressed the grandfather of his current patron with his great talents for metal work. As a young apprentice, he was the one who got all the worst work, so of course he was the man down in the pit who pulled down on the bottom of the two-man saw.

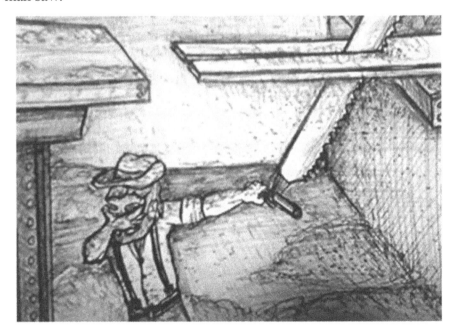

The pit man had the dirtiest job at the mill, for the sawdust fell straight down on him with every downward stroke of the blade. There was no breeze in the musty pit, so in minutes, he was covered with sawdust from head to toe. Even though he took three dunkings a day in the nearby stream, he still had sawdust in every crevasse of his body. It was why, to this day, old August would only used riven planks to make anything. It was his contribution to the pit men of the world, to keep the demand for sawn planks to a minimum.

For several years, though, he had been aware of a new machine that eliminated the man in the pits, by allowing the top man to do all the work by himself. Because of his experience as a youth, he paid keen attention to how that machine was constructed, since it paroled so many young men from a purgatory of filth and bad health. The interesting thing about that machine is that it multiplied the force of the one sawyer by extending his arms through levers. An especially long lever of iron, called a pitman arm, did the work that a man formerly had to do. The pitman arm was attached to a powerful spring, and since the entire mechanism was too ungainly to fit into the pit, it was constructed in such a way as to remain outside. The machine was therefore much larger than the workplace, and had to be built outside it. Could the same be done for the spring of his wind gun lock?

To his great joy he discovered that it could! The entire lock had to be turned inside-out to work this way, but old Bidderman was so overjoyed with the solution that he hardly seemed to notice the extra work. When he was finished he admired what the world had never before seen—a wind gun with the workings of the lock on the outside!

Naturally he tested the finished piece time after time, and to his amazement he discovered it worked even better than he had dared to hope. Fully 15 powerful shots could be gotten from a single butt of wind. Even the last of these was powerful enough to bury the lead ball so deep in his door that just its tip could be seen.

All the while he was working on the gun, he was also fashioning the associated pieces that must accompany it. The condensing syringe he made was larger and more effective than the one that came with the gun from the Low Country. And the mold he made to make the lead balls was outfitted with ebony handles to keep the person's hands safe from the terrific heat of the molten lead.

All of these pieces he made to fit into a finely finished wooden case that he lined with a deep brown material. Each piece had its own compartment and the whole outfit took on the look of fine jewelry. Just wait until the young baron first saw it!

That opportunity came within the next week. He called at the great hall and found the nobleman available, so the two men retired to the inner garden where they could be alone. He presented the younger man with the dark walnut case in which his treasure was housed. There was the butt in one section; the barrel and lock in another—the longest, which ran the full length of the case; the condensing syringe and a separate set of handles with which to pump it; the ball mold with its beautiful dark wooden handles; a set of spare horn seals for replacement when the gun started to loose force; an oil bottle for lubrication of the seal between the butt and lock; and one more section. The final section was covered by a closely fitted lid, and contained balls already cast, plus the small key to lock the case. The entire presentation was as breathtaking as the very idea of the gun, itself.

The baron found himself without words to express his gratitude. This was so far beyond his expectations that it was almost something else, indeed! Oh, how he would lord it over his cousin when next they met!

Then, he chanced to notice the number three impressed on top of the lock. "Herr Bidderman, what does this number signify?"

"My lord, you were so concerned that the Emperor would try to steal this gun from you if ever he learned of its existence that I devised a way to prevent that from happening. I put the number three on this lock because I am going to make two more guns especially for the Emperor. They will be a matched pair of the most exquisite beauty anyone has ever seen. No one will have a pair of guns, wind or firelock, that can compare to what I will make for him. And, they will be the last royal commission I will ever undertake—if I live long enough to finish it."

"I am astounded, my old friend. What gave you such an idea?"

"My lord, I know that my time on earth will soon come to an end. I have no apprentice to whom I can pass even a fraction of the secrets I possess, so they will perish with me. If I were to die with such a speculative commission in progress…"

"...the Emperor will break down the gates of heaven and hell to find a craftsman to finish the project! He will build his own guns and leave mine alone! By Jove—what a plan!"

"Yes, my lord, I think I out-foxed him this time."

True to his premonition, August Bidderman closed his eyes for the final time four months later. He died in his sleep, apparently without a struggle of any kind. The baron laid him to rest in his family's own plot in the yard of the chapel that served the north end of the valley. The entire village of Prostl turned out for the funeral, and there wasn't a dry eye present.

The Emperor never did learn of the existence of Von Eiger's fabulous wind gun, but the cousin from the Low Countries certainly did! He was consumed with jealousy after shooting the piece one afternoon, so Von Eiger had to let him take it back to Antwerp to have it copied.

There wasn't a craftsman willing to undertake the work in Antwerp, but in the city of Liege there was a man who said he could do it. He kept the gun for almost a full year before returning it to the cousin, who raced across Europe to return it to the baron—so long had it been out of his sight.

The copy proved to work as well as the original, so the workman in Liege began making more of them for his other patrons. Soon, other men in the town copied the design, and they began turning up everywhere. Several centuries later, there would be such a proliferation of the pattern that some experts would come to believe that it had originated in Liege.

The baron's gun was handed down for two more generations, until the dissolution of the family estate in 1796, when it was sold at auction to a wealthy merchant from Ingolstadt. He kept it for 20 more years before selling it to cover a loss in his business. The gun's whereabouts were lost from that time until the end of World War I, when it was rediscovered in the ruins of an estate in western France. The liberator, an English officer, took it home with him as a souvenir, but to keep curious eyes from discerning its presence during transit, he left the case where he found it and took the gun in pieces.

His family later sold the gun at a weapons fair in Birmingham, in 1956. Then, in 1968, the gun was documented in a short article in a British airgun magazine. This brought it to the attention of a wealthy American collector who flew to England and bought it from the owner.

In 1989, the gun was again sold at a gun show in Dallas, Texas. By that time, there was only the gun. All the other accessories, including the pump, had been stripped away by the indifference of casual owners over the centuries. It still fetched $8,500 because of its great elegance and beauty. The sights, which the maker believed to be made from elephant tusks, were actually discovered to be mammoth ivory—obtained from frozen carcasses recovered by Russian expeditions in the 18th century. They survive to the present day.

Today, the outside lock air gun made by August Bidderman for Baron Von Eiger resides in a collection in the United States. Although the story of the piece sounds complete, its history is still unfolding. The great care with which it was constructed has given the airgun a kind of near immortality. Anyone who possesses it for a time will do his utmost to conserve it.

The valve seals have been replaced with modern synthetic components, which, while they give no more power, at least seal it so well that sperm whale oil is no longer required.

August Bidderman died in the year 1727, but his masterpieces still live on. The one and only wind gun he ever made is perhaps the final epitaph for the man whose name has been all but erased from the pages of history. It is a work of art that inspires all who see it to preserve the most tangible part that remains of the old master.

About the Author

Tom Gaylord is an internationally known airgun author, speaker and personality. He has written and edited for print, radio and television, both in the U.S. and Europe. He wrote *The Airgun Letter* newsletter for nine years, and was the editor and principal writer of *Airgun Revue* magazine. In 2002 he helped found, edit and write *Airgun Illustrated*— America's only newsstand airgun publication. He wrote the *Beeman RI Supermagnum Air Rifle* book. He has advised the National Rifle Association, Daisy Manufacturing Company, the Crosman Corporation, Leapers, Predator Pellets, AirForce Airguns, and numerous other members of the airgun industry. He conceived and helped to develop the highly successful Benjamin Discovery pneumatic rifle, the Walther Dominator field target rifle and the RWS Diana droop-compensating scope base. Tom appears regularly on *American Airgunner*, where he was given the title, The Godfather Of Airguns. Visit his website at www.thegodfatherofairguns.com.

Printed in the USA
CPSIA information can be obtained
at www.ICGtesting.com
CBHW020307100824
12842CB00031B/177